I0595035

Phantasm

Starlight Investigations - Book 3

Marnie Atwell

Copyright © 2020 Marnie Atwell

No part of this publication may be reproduced or transmitted in any form or by any means, electronic or mechanical, including photocopying, recording, storage in an information retrieval system, or otherwise, without the prior written permission of the author.

This is a work of fiction. Names, characters, places, incidents and dialogues are products of the author's imagination or are used fictitiously. Any resemblance to actual people, living or dead, events or locales is entirely coincidental.

The Starlight Investigation Series is written by an Australian author who uses Australian English.

First Edition printed in Australia 2020

ISBN: 978-0-6483158-7-2

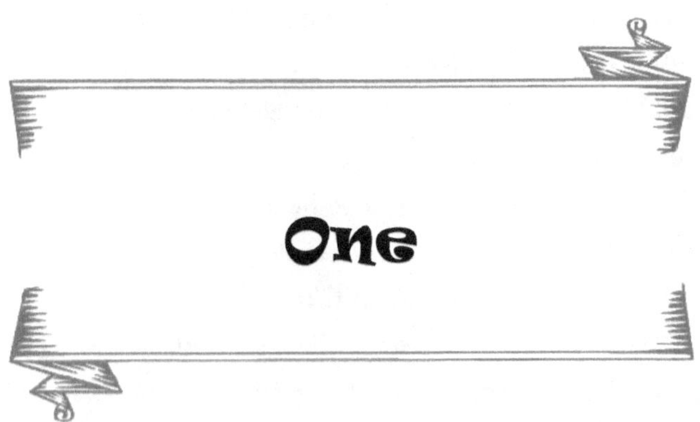

One

The frat house was in full swing by the time Chandra made her appearance. She approached the front door of the two-storey building with a smile on her face and a sway to her hips. Her black leather pants, which were tucked into a pair of black knee-high boots, left nothing to the imagination. They hugged her body like a second skin. Her apricot coloured top was also form-fitting with short-capped sleeves and a heart-shaped neckline.

She eyed the doorman appreciatively, enjoying the way his muscles flexed when he caught sight of her approach. "Hello there, handsome," she purred, running her hand over his chest.

He gazed into her dark brown eyes, feeling as though they were pulling him deeper into their depths. "I was beginning to think you weren't coming," he murmured, leaning in for a kiss.

She chuckled with happiness, her eyes sparkling with mischief. "How could I stand being in there, when I know you have been relegated to guard duty out here?" She pouted her lips and pressed herself closer to him. Tilting her head further, she gently pressed her lips to the underside of his chin, revelling in the shudder that passed through his body.

"You are such a tease," he groaned, grabbing her beneath the arms and lifting her off her feet. His mouth came down on hers, claiming them for his own. She wrapped her legs around his midriff and crushed her chest to his own. Her arms wrapped securely around his neck.

"Knock it off, you two," the president of Delta Nu fraternity growled, punching his buddy on the arm. Chandra and Lauchlen broke off their kiss to gaze at the blonde footballer. "You weren't supposed to arrive for another hour," he accused.

"I was bored and lonely," Chandra replied with a sulky tone.

"You. Lonely?" he scoffed. "There is a line, a mile long," he spread his arms wide, "of men waiting to take Lauchie's place."

"And what do you think Lauchlen would do to these men if I were to take them up on their offer?" she quizzed him.

"Beat them to a pulp, I should imagine."

"And what would that do to your team, when Coach is forced to suspend him from playing?"

"It would make it harder to win the next game."

"Exactly," she grinned, closing her eyes as Lauchlen's mouth found the sensitive spot below her left ear. She continued a little breathlessly, "Why don't you find somebody else to watch the door so me and my boy here can have a bit of privacy?"

"That's not how it works, Chandra, and you know it. Lauchlen has another hour of guard duty. After that, he is all yours. You can either move inside and partake of the festivities, or you can leave and find something else to occupy your time."

"Don't go," Lauchlen begged. "I want you here the minute my shift is over."

"As you wish," she slid down his body until her feet met the floor.

After claiming her mouth once more, Lauchlen watched her enter the lion's den, knowing she was more than capable of looking after herself. Chandra felt the weight of his stare and smiled. It had been a long time since she had felt the pull of her heartstrings towards a human. She was looking forward to getting to know him better.

Chandra knew the house inside out. She had been there many times before but reminded herself she was supposed to be relatively new to her surroundings. She took a deep breath, then looked around uncertainly. Chandra drew attention wherever she went and was not left on her own for long. She noticed a couple of groups converging on her. Both were mixed sexes, made up of footballers and cheerleaders. She didn't want to get stuck with either. She was hunting a monster.

Chandra glanced around looking for something she could use to divert the attention of those approaching. Even with her heels, she was shorter than most of those in attendance. Glancing up, she saw a group of women leaning against the rails on the second level. Pretending to know one of them, she raised her hand in greeting and yelled, "Marcia, so good to see you. I'm coming up."

With an apologetic glance to the two groups, she made her way towards the staircase then climbed to the next floor. Once there, she bypassed the women who appeared confused, and made her way into the president's bedroom; a place she knew would be empty. He would be downstairs courting the ladies, seeming attainable, when in fact, he was in a serious relationship with the line-backer.

Chandra placed her hands on the wall and allowed her energy to connect with the structure. She encouraged it to pulsate, searching the interior for that which was not human. With a frustrated sigh, she let her arm fall to her side. The creature was not present. She would need to move on to one of the other three fraternities holding parties that evening. Feeling disappointed, she turned towards the door and screamed as one hand covered her mouth while an arm wrapped itself around her waist.

She charged her body with electrical energy and focused it towards the appendages gripping her without permission. A being appeared in front of her as the assailant behind her screeched with pain. Although she knew he was hurting, she felt his limbs tightening on her body. Before her mind could register the identity of her visitor, she felt herself falling backwards through space.

Her eyes widened in fear, before blazing with fury. She was being abducted, and she'd be damned if she was going to take that lying down. As the pair arrived on Australian soil, Chandra's body morphed into that of a rattlesnake. She faced Guardian Manuel and performed the dance of a predator.

Manuel gazed at her in horror. He slowly lowered his arms, praying that she wouldn't strike. He hoped Elden appeared quickly to help him contain the dilemma they found themselves in. Preferably before

Chandra bit him, or the tornado bearing down on them picked him up and spat him out.

Elden arrived a couple of minutes later, swiftly assessing the situation. "Chandra, I need your attention," he said, stepping forward to garner the snake's focus. She felt the vibration through the Earth and shifted her head to place Elden in view. "There is a storm coming, Chandra. It is going to hurt a lot of people. We need your help to defuse the situation." He watched her sway and swallowed uncomfortably. "Your sister, Rochelle, is hurting, Chandra. She is affecting the weather. She needs you."

He pointed to a woman lying a few metres away. She was on her side with her head tucked into her hands. Her heartfelt sobs were lost to the rising squall. The snake's head turned further, her tongue flicking out to taste her surroundings. Elden and Manuel gasped with fright as the reptile began to move. They stayed still and waited with bated breath.

She passed them both to attend to her sister's needs. As soon as she was within reach, Chandra became human and snuggled her body into her sister's back. She placed her arm over Rochelle's side and tucked her in close. "I can't believe you are alive," Chandra sobbed. "I thought you had died in The Cleanse." Chandra opened herself to mind-link. The sensations she felt when they connected, made her own heart splinter.

Chandra closed her eyes as Rochelle's pain hit her. Tears squeezed out from beneath her eyelids, and her lungs ached with each expansion and contraction. A heaviness settled in her chest, and her lips quivered. '*Sleep,*' she said from within Rochelle's mind.

The air pressure lowered further. Elden carefully lowered his hand to her arm. "Chandra, the storm is going to hurt a lot of people unless you can get Rochelle to stop."

"How am I supposed to take Rochelle's pain away? Who has ever loved anyone as much as Rochelle has loved Toranthian? Five hundred years, they were a couple. Friends for longer than that. There is no stopping what you have allowed coming to pass."

"We did not turn him into a vampire," Elden reminded her.

"No, but you allowed the vampire to return to Earth so that she could hunt him. You might as well have injected him with the virus yourself."

"That's not fair. The Pegasus warned Queen Adair not to interfere with Destiny's plan."

"Well, Destiny can go . . ."

"Please, Chandra. Can *you* stop the storm?" Manuel butted in, hoping to calm her emotions.

"Why should I help you?"

"You took an oath to save the humans. They are in danger."

"I took an oath to save them from creatures, not the weather."

"A Gatherer that takes the life of a human, intentional or not, will be put to death. Please don't put us in a position where we have to kill your sister."

Chandra placed all of her energy into counteracting her sister's power. She was able to dissipate the storm before the tornado touched down. The hailstones were broken down to their elements and the clouds lightened until they disappeared altogether. "There. It is done. Now leave us," Chandra commanded.

"Let us take you where you will have some privacy," Elden implored.

"No, thanks. I am quite capable of finding a place for myself," Chandra said, getting to her feet and lifting her sister into her arms.

Rochelle opened her eyes and focussed on her sister's. Her eyes widened with surprise. "Chandra?"

"Yeah, Sis. It's me."

Rochelle lay her head on Chandra's shoulder, wrapping her arms more tightly around her sister's neck. The sadness contained in Rochelle's heart was overwhelming her once more. Clouds began to build swiftly. Chandra wondered how Rochelle was able to fight the sleep command she had been given.

Not knowing what else to do, Chandra shared the burden with her sister, taking half of the pain into herself. She hoped that between them, they would be able to manage the agony to the extent that would allow Rochelle to keep from affecting the weather, placing human lives in danger.

Chandra glared at Elden, "I was hunting a Shocker Demon in LA when you so rudely kidnapped me. Someone will need to take over to protect the college students," she said sarcastically. "You won't be able to separate us now that we know the other lives."

"I know," he said as he opened a portal to Mystique.

Elden and Manuel looked at each other with something close to panic in their eyes. "Have we done the right thing?" Manuel asked.

"I don't know," Elden frowned as they stepped through the doorway and disappeared.

Chandra looked at Rochelle with teary eyes. "Where would you like me to take you, Rochelle?"

An image of a place popped into Rochelle's mind. Chandra strode towards Rochelle's car, placed her gently in the passenger side and strapped her in. She sat in the driver's seat, looking for a button that would start the car.

Rochelle gave the start command bringing a smile to Chandra's face. "Sweet," she drawled in response. Rochelle's mouth rose slightly at the corners, but not enough to put the shine back in her eyes.

Two

A cursory glance was all Chandra afforded the outside of the cabin. It was small, one-storey and constructed of wood. She carried her sister to the front door and used her ability to control nature to unlock the door. With a gentle tap of the foot, the door swung open, and she walked inside.

The mind-link between them had informed Chandra that Rochelle had never set foot inside the place. Chandra was surprised to discover the cabin was dust-free. She pursed her lips, scrunching them to the right. She was pretty sure a quick look in the cold box and cupboards would show the place had been prepared in advance. Why had Rochelle suggested they come here? Who did the cottage belong to?

"Where are we?" she asked.

Rochelle sighed, "Our place. Toren was building this to celebrate our anniversary."

"You didn't help him?"

"It was supposed to be a secret," Rochelle rolled her eyes. "But he was so excited by it, he kept bringing it to the forefront of his thoughts."

Chandra's eyes flashed with understanding as she scanned the area for a comfortable place to set Rochelle down. The lounge was highly inviting, made from white leather and more than big enough for the two of them to sit comfortably. However, it was still covered in plastic, and not the least bit manageable while Rochelle nestled sadly in her arms. The wooden-framed chairs in the kitchen, also covered in plastic, had plush padded seats with matching inserts embedded into the backrests.

Walking towards the back of the cottage, she found a working bathroom and a couple of bedrooms. Thinking that a smaller bed would be better for someone who had just become single, Chandra veered left and lay Rochelle on top of a bedspread with a picture of a wolf.

Its grey and white fur looked soft and fluffy. The head was tipped slightly to the side in an inquisitive pose. The eyes were yellow, intelligent beacons commanding the surveyor's attention. Chandra imagined the comfort such a creature would provide at a time such as this and found herself beginning to transform into a wolf.

"Stay with me," Rochelle pleaded, sensing her sister's intentions. She sat up and grasped Chandra's hand in her own. "I don't need a slobbering mutt to console me. I need to see my sister. Why has it taken three thousand years for you to show yourself to me?"

"I thought you were dead, Rochelle. The Guardians said you perished in The Cleanse."

"*That* is what they told me about *you*," Rochelle nodded, wiping the tears from her eyes. "I can't believe I trusted them."

"Yeah," Chandra said, squeezing her hand. "They give with one hand and take away with the other. I'm really sorry about Toranthian."

"You know about him?"

"Only what I have garnered from linking minds with you. You loved him a lot, didn't you?"

"I still do," Rochelle admitted.

"That is not going to stop because he is gone," Chandra stated.

"He's not just gone, Chandra. He's a vampire."

"I know. I saw that, too."

"They said I can save him," her voice barely above a whisper.

"I beg your pardon," Chandra stiffened her spine. "They expect you to be the one to put him down?"

"No, they expect me to reverse the process."

"That's not possible, Sis," Chandra placed her other hand on Rochelle's cheek, gripping her hand a little tighter.

"The Pegasus' have a plan. They see things we can't see."

Chandra was flabbergasted that they would play with Rochelle's emotions in such a way. If that were true, the Pegasus' would have stopped him from being turned in the first place. She hadn't thought much of the royals and guardians before. Her feelings towards them just slid another few notches. "I hope they are right," she said with some truth. "Are you hungry?"

"No," Rochelle shook her head. "Thirsty, though."

"I'll rustle us up a cup of coffee," Chandra rose elegantly, attempting to release her sister's hand. Rochelle's grip tightened as she jumped to her feet.

"I'm not letting you out of my sight," she explained.

Chandra smiled, "I'm not going anywhere. Wild dragons couldn't fly me away from your side. Why don't you just lie there and rest for a while?"

"I would feel a lot better if we remained in the same room."

"You're a Battle Star. What are you afraid of?"

"That they'll take you away, too."

Chandra laughed. "Not going to happen." She pulled a black coloured belt, made from the same fabric as the battle suits they wore, from her pocket and held it up for Rochelle to see. It had a titanium buckle with a Pegasus emblem. "I lifted this from Guardian Manuel."

"What is it?" Rochelle inquired.

"I believe it is the device they use to create portals here on Earth. Can you imagine how easy it would be to gather creatures if we could move instantaneously from one place to another? This device would be a game-changer."

"Indeed it would," Rochelle said, reaching her hand out to rub the cold metal. "How do you think it works?"

"I believe Guardian Elden depressed the back of the buckle with his thumb."

"Should we try it?"

"Maybe later," Chandra led Rochelle to a round wooden table, placing the two cups on the uncovered surface. She pulled out the chairs and stripped the protective plastic away before taking a seat. She waited for Rochelle to become comfortable before saying, "I want to know what you have been up to."

"I can't talk about him, Chandra. My heart is broken. I don't know if it will ever heal."

"Of course it will, in time. You need to allow yourself time to grieve."

"How can I grieve with the knowledge he lives, as a monster. A creature that preys on the blood of humans. A thing that looks like my Toren yet is not."

"You must mourn for the loss of his humanity. For what you have shared together that can no longer continue. You will not move forward until you have done so."

"There is no moving forward," Rochelle's anguished voice matched her eyes. "I am in limbo until it is time to do what must be done to reverse the vampirism flowing through his veins." Rochelle rose from the chair and stalked towards the hallway.

"Where are you going?"

"I need to finish my job."

"You are hunting?"

"Not exactly. I have been tasked with convincing a phantasm to return to his body."

"Why? Is he a danger to society?"

"No, he's just a scared, confused teenager in need of guidance."

"So how did you become involved?"

"You wouldn't believe me if I told you."

"Try me," Chandra said, pointing to the vacated chair.

Rochelle sighed. She needed to keep busy, or she was going to lose her mind. The last thing she wanted to do at that time was to sit and talk some more with her sister. There would be plenty of time for that later, once her emotions had stabilised.

"I can't do this," Rochelle growled, frustration lacing her voice.

"It will only take a few minutes," Chandra encouraged. "Give me your hand. I will get what I need through mind-link."

"You don't need to connect to me to get information."

"I am trying to offer you my support. You are not alone, Rochelle. Let me be your rock and help you complete your mission. It will be over twice as fast if we work together."

"Fine," Rochelle stated, too tired to argue. She sat in the chair and held out her hand.

Chandra gripped it gently with her own and smiled. "I won't dig any deeper than the surface. Put whatever you want to share at the forefront of your consciousness."

"I know how this works, Chandra," Rochelle rolled her eyes.

"We haven't seen each other for three thousand years. I want you to know you can still trust me like you could back then."

"I won't stop trusting you until you give me a reason to."

Chandra closed her eyes and opened them. With a deep breath, she said, "Let's begin."

"Let me show you what I have discovered so far."

Chandra's brown eyes gazed into Rochelle's grey ones. Within seconds, they were connected on a deeper level, their sight focused on the events in Rochelle's head. Varying emotions flashed unseen across Chandra's face as the images poured in, starting from two weeks ago.

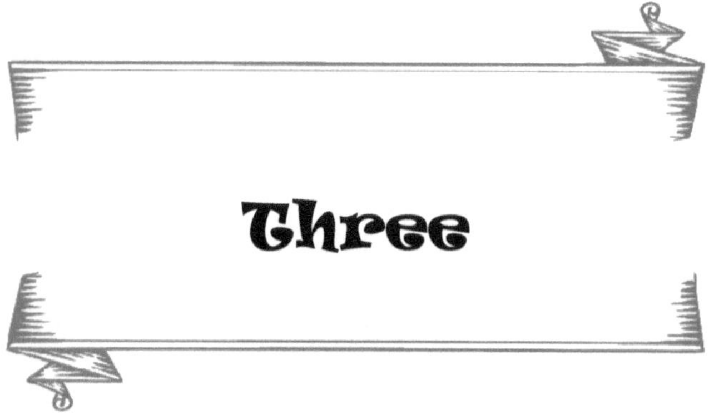

Three

A shadow fell upon the classroom, muting the brightness inside. The senior students cast their eyes towards the windows and gasped in awe at the view. A cluster of white, wispy clouds that had begun forming thirty minutes prior had transformed into a swirling mass of black and green.

Lightning dashed across the sky, creating a deep rumble throughout the suburb. A stray bolt of lightning descended, aiming itself at a healthy gum that grew outside their window. The students jumped in their seats and screamed with fright as a flash of lightning lit the room, and a deafening crack of thunder threatened to shake the place apart. Even Mr Warren believed the Heavens had explicitly targeted the school. He was actually contemplating the idea that the end of the world was nigh.

"All right students, I don't want you to panic, but those closest to the windows ought to close them. The rest of you, under your desks, NOW!" he screamed above the howling wind, then proceeded to climb under a desk himself.

"Absolutely useless," Cameron muttered, walking to the windows to close those that were still open because his classmates had hidden under their desks. "You're an adult and supposed to protect us, not the other way around." Once he'd completed the task, he returned to his designated seat and climbed beneath the desk.

"Brave move," his friend Xavier commented.

"You would have done it if I hadn't beaten you to it," he grunted.

Xavier pulled out his phone to connect to the Internet. "Looks pretty bad on B.O.M."

"And what does the Bureau of Meteorology have to report?" Cameron asked.

"Nothing good. There are warnings everywhere. Large hailstones, flash flooding, extreme wind conditions . . ." his voice trailed off. He showed Cameron the radar images and then clicked the screen to gain a broader view. "Looks like more storms are developing behind it."

"Maybe we shouldn't go to Wotomba this afternoon."

Xavier agreed. "I reckon this will be going on all night by the looks of it. Not safe weather to be travelling in."

"You know Adrian will disagree. He'll say something like *Dude, it's only twenty to three. This will blow over in half an hour, and the sun will be shining again.*"

Xavier looked at Cameron, with an impressed expression. "You sounded just like him."

"Yeah? Well, you know I'm right," he shrugged.

"If he wants to drive to Wotomba, he'll be going on his own. None of the other guys will take the risk of running into something like this on the streets. Considering Wotomba is in the same direction as these other developing storms, I can pretty well guarantee they will decline the invitation of a ride."

"He's not going to be happy."

"No, he won't, but I doubt he will go on his own. Why don't we suggest tomorrow morning instead."

"I can't. My sister has an exam, and I agreed to take care of her daughter for her."

"What time will she be finished?"

"Around eleven. Do you want to come with me to a three-year-old's birthday party? It'll be a load of fun."

"Hell no! You're on your own there, bro," Xavier smirked.

"Thanks a bunch."

"Not a problem," Xavier replied, as his smile widened.

"Yeah, for you."

The storm continued to lash the windows as the boys fell into a comfortable silence. It was a quarter past three when the school released them to make their way home. The guys usually caught a lift with Adrian but decided to give that a miss in case he decided to be stupid and drove to Wotomba instead of their homes. Knowing it would take longer to get home, they didn't want to get caught up in a discussion with Adrian. Xavier sent him a text. **Walking home. More storms coming. Giving Wotomba a miss. How about tomorrow arvo instead?** He pocketed the phone, then waited for his brother, Bradley, to appear at the front gate.

Cameron didn't want to hang around, so he said his goodbyes and began the fifteen-minute walk home, taking in the carnage as he went. There were fallen branches all over the place, and hail half the size of a ping-pong ball still littered the ground beneath his feet. He could feel the cold seeping through the soles of his sneakers as his feet failed to crush the ice as he stepped on it. *'It must have been cold up there for the ice to be so hard in the middle,'* he thought but wasn't really sure. He hadn't paid enough attention to the meteorology unit they'd completed in science. His interests lay in anatomy, more so human than other animals or plants.

He enjoyed the walk home, even though the chill in the air caused the hair on his body to stand on end. There was a crispness to the atmosphere that wasn't usually experienced at that time of year. Hot winds and humidity generally sent rivers of sweat cascading down his body. The temperature of the afternoon invigorated Cameron. He wished he didn't feel obligated to travel with the guys.

He appreciated that they had brought him into their friend group when his brother-in-law had passed away three months ago. Well, everyone except Adrian, who didn't really like him much. But when Xavier, Bradley, and Tommy all voted to help him out in his time of need, Adrian decided to keep the peace and let his own feelings about Cameron slide. So Adrian picked him up every morning, drove him home every afternoon, and included him in their social gatherings.

It'd be good to have some time to himself occasionally. His father worked for a brokerage company that paid enough money that Cameron's mother didn't have to work. She pottered around the house doing housework during school hours and took great delight in getting under his feet when he came home. She asked all sorts of embarrassing questions and like a dog with a bone, wouldn't stop until he went to his room slamming the door. At that point, she would begin yelling at him about his lack of manners and remind him there was a no-closed-door policy in the house. By that time, both their nerves were shot, and his father walked into a battlefield wishing he was back at work.

After some consideration, Cameron realised his father had begun coming home a little later each week. When he examined his memories, Cameron was alarmed to find his father's new routine had taken place shortly after David's funeral had been held.

His heart broke a little further as it became apparent to him that he had not offered any form of support to his parents over their loss. *Time to do something about that,'* he thought. They had loved David as much as they loved him, choosing not to distinguish between son and son-in-law.

Before entering his home, he made sure to wipe his feet carefully on the mat. He didn't want to upset his mother by dragging mud and debris through the house. He crossed the threshold into the hallway, stepped out of his shoes and placed them on the rack.

Next, he removed his blazer and hung it on the nearest hook to the door. Loosening his tie, he continued toward the kitchen. "Mum, are you home?" he called, surprised she hadn't rushed to his side the moment he stepped inside the house. When he arrived at the kitchen door, he discovered the reason for her silence. His mother lay in a heap on the floor.

Cameron reached for the light switch then rushed to her side, tugging at the hem of her dress to protect her modesty. He gently tapped her on the cheek, "Mum, Mum, can you hear me? Open your eyes."

"Cameron?" she groaned.

"Yes, Mum, it's me. Are you hurting anywhere?"

"No. What happened?" she asked, blinking because the light was stinging her eyes.

"I was hoping you could tell me. Do you know where you are?"

"No, where am I?"

"In the kitchen. Do you remember what happened?"

"I had a vision," she exclaimed.

Cameron rolled his eyes and groaned. '*Not this again,*' he thought. "You must have fallen and hit your head," he attempted to investigate.

Karen raised her hand and swatted him. "Get away with you."

"Be still, Mother," he said, holding her hand with his own, and using his other hand to check for bumps, cuts, and blood to her head.

"Keeley is scared, Cameron. She is blindfolded and scared. You need to keep watch and protect her. You *will* make sure she is okay, won't you, dear?"

"Of course I will, Mum. You are probably worried about her playing '*Pin the Tail on the Donkey*' at the party tomorrow. Don't fret. Either Melissa or I will be there with her, depending on what time they play the game." Then muttered to himself, '*If they play at all.*'

"And Cameron? Be careful."

"Come on, let's get you to the doctor."

"There's no need for that."

"You've had a bump to the head," he said, not knowing whether she had or not. His only comfort was the fact that his mother didn't know, either. "It doesn't hurt to have this checked out. Besides, Doctor Gordon would be furious with me if you had a relapse due to an undiagnosed problem."

"You worry too much, Cameron," she said softly. Karen patted his arm then rose to her feet with his help. She was a bit unsteady and used him to lean on. Cameron grabbed her handbag from the table and found the car keys in the front pocket. As he drove to the medical centre, he gritted his teeth against her tirade.

"You shouldn't be driving. You are supposed to have a capable driver on their open licence with you in the car. I can hardly be called capable considering you're rushing me to the doctors to get checked for a head injury. What if the cops pull us over? You could lose your learner's licence, and then where will you be? Back to square one, I tell you."

Luckily, they made it to the medical centre without seeing any police. He was glad to find that she was in good health. The doctor believed she hadn't sustained any injuries during her fall other than a bruise on her leg that she hadn't even known was there until he pressed it with his finger. When they arrived home, Karen took great pleasure in relating her adventure to her husband. He replied, "That's nice, dear," and then checked the house, inside and out, for storm damage.

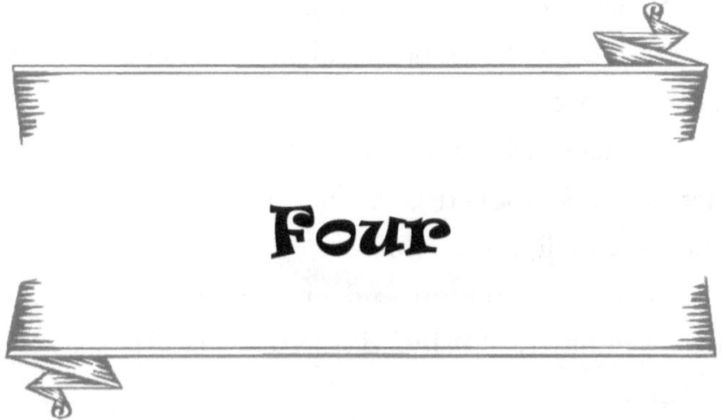

Four

Cameron surveyed the options before him feeling entirely out of his depth. The garments laid before him were of the same quality and lengths. Surely, any one of them would be suitable attire for the party that was taking place in a couple of hours. But then, what did he know? At seventeen years of age, he didn't have all the answers yet.

"This one?" Keeley asked, holding a different outfit against her body so he could see what it would look like on.

"I don't know, Keeley. They all look lovely. Which one do *you* want to wear?"

"I don't know," she cried dramatically, then proceeded to throw herself on the bed, wrinkling the dresses she had placed there so carefully moments before.

Cameron was horrified. How could a birthday party for a three-year-old, cause so much angst? "Why are you so worried about picking the right dress? You will be beautiful in whichever one you decide to wear, Keeley."

"Manda not likes me much now," Keeley sat up on her bed and looked at Cameron. "If I look pwetty, she might talk me again."

"To me," Cameron said in automatic response to her grammar. "Why doesn't Amanda like you anymore?"

"I cwied when Daddy died. She not likes sooks."

Cameron felt a flash of anger but quickly reined it in. The girls were clearly not capable of understanding a complex issue such as death and the processes involved in dealing with the emotions that arose from such a tragedy. He looked at her solemn face and felt his heart break a little more. She appeared extremely fragile, which wasn't surprising. It had only been a few months since David's death. Her blonde hair fell back behind her shoulders as she looked up at him with pleading blue eyes. Her hands fidgeted as she waited anxiously for him to help her make the right decision.

"Is there a theme for the party?" he questioned.

"We be pwincesses," she squealed with delight.

"Well then, that makes the decision easy." Cameron walked to the wardrobe and picked out the dress he had bought for her the day before her father died. Cameron and Keeley's mother, Melissa, had decided to put it away so that she would not associate it with her dad's death. "What about this one?"

Keeley looked at the dress, her small eyes widened with unsuppressed pleasure. She jumped off the bed and raced to stand before Cameron. He held it up to her so that she could see herself in the mirrored door. The sleeves of the dress came down to her elbows and were finished with white lace. The bodice of the dress was styled like most princess' outfits on the Disney channel, and the skirt of the dress billowed out in true princess style, finishing at her ankles with white lace poking out beneath. The material was pale apricot which complimented her blonde locks and the tan colour of her skin to perfection.

"This is nice but doesn't have a picture of a pwincess on it. Whose is it?"

"Nobody's, Keeley. That is why it is so special."

"How so?"" she asked.

"It is a Princess Keeley dress. Because you are wearing it, it doesn't need a picture on the bodice."

"What's a bodice?"

"The part where your chest and tummy is."

Keeley looked at her reflection again. She loved the dress but was still not convinced that she should wear it. Maybe it would be better to choose one of her garments that had a picture of Princess Elsa or Snow White on it instead.

"Shoes?"

Cameron looked inside her wardrobe and plucked a pair of white sandals from the shelf. He laid them on the floor, "What about these?"

"Hmm," Keeley replied, sticking her pointer finger in her mouth. Always a sign she was in deep thought. "They not talls," she finally stated.

"Talls?" Cameron queried.

"She means high heels," Melissa walked into the room.

"Oh," Cameron nodded with a smile.

"Mamma," Keeley squealed, dropping the dress and launching herself at her mother.

Melissa grinned, while Cameron picked her dress up with a scowl. "Never mind it wrinkling," he huffed.

"Oh, Cameron, you are going to make some girl very happy one day," his sister laughed.

"How do you know I haven't already?" he answered.

"I don't remember being invited to the wedding."

"Who said anything about getting married?" he choked.

"Never mind," Melissa snorted. "They've rescheduled my exam to next week due to damage caused by the storm yesterday. I'm sorry for stuffing you around today, but is there any possibility of you taking care of Keeley next Saturday?"

"Of course, Melissa. I love spending time with her. I'm usually here anyway."

"Yes, but your exams start the week after. Will you have enough time to study?"

"I could sit my exams today and pass with flying colours, Liss. Don't sweat it."

"How are you, Sweet Pea?" Melissa turned her attention to Keeley.

"Gweat! Uncle Camwon picked out a dwess and shoes, and I all set."

"Really?" Melissa raised her eyebrows. "You don't want to go shopping to get something else?" Melissa thought about all the things she had purchased in the past few months to keep Keeley happy so that *she* could come to terms with her husband's passing.

"We could get a bag?" Keeley smiled mischievously.

"Don't need to. Here's the perfect accessory for your outfit," Melissa responded, bringing the arm she had kept hidden behind her back to the front, which held a small white clutch.

"Oh," Keeley gasped. "Perfect." She ran over to Cameron and started pushing him towards the door. "Out now, I need to get dwessed."

Cameron couldn't help but giggle. He stood his ground and watched as she puffed and panted. "Uncle Camwon," she whined.

"It's okay, Poppet. I just want a hug and a kiss before I go."

"So you're not going to come with us?" Melissa questioned.

"No. I had no problems standing in for you when you had something important to do. But a birthday party for rugrats goes way above the duties of a favourite uncle."

Laughing, Melissa said, "You're her only uncle."

"Always the favourite," he grinned. "Sorry, Liss. I have a better offer."

"And what would that be?" she asked as Keeley gave him a big hug and a kiss on the cheek.

"Some friends and I are going roller skating at Wotomba. It will be the last chance we get before sitting our final exams, preparing for our Formal and embarking on new adventures."

"I see," Melissa said. "Well then, we won't keep you from your pleasantries. Have fun and be safe."

"I will. Have a good time yourself." He laughed when Melissa responded by rolling her eyes. "You know about the rift between Keeley and Amanda?"

Melissa nodded, "Yeah, I know about it. Hopefully, I will have a chance to speak to Amanda's mum and get it all sorted out. Keeley, don't put your party dress on yet, it's too early. Put on your yellow panda shirt and black shorts, then we'll go downstairs for breakfast, okay?"

Cameron hugged Melissa and walked out of the room, leaving them to get ready. He hoped Melissa would be successful in her endeavours to repair the friendship between the youngsters. Losing David had been hard on him, too. David had become the brother he never had, and his death had left Cameron feeling bereft and bewildered. His fishing and camping buddy gone in an instant, leaving a gaping hole where love and friendship had once been.

He jumped on his bike and headed for Adrian's place. Cameron wondered what reaction he would get when he got there. Xavier had told Adrian that Cameron was busy that morning so of course, that was when Adrian had decided to leave for Wotomba.

Halfway to Adrian's, Cameron realised he had forgotten to tell Melissa about his mother's vision and his promise to protect Keeley. He brought his bike to a stop beneath a shady tree and pulled out his phone. She answered on the second ring.

"Is everything all right, Cameron?"

"Yeah, I just forgot to mention Mum had one of her *visions* again."

"What about this time?"

"Keeley. Mum said she becomes scared when she is blindfolded."

"Oh, yeah, she told me about that last night and told me you wouldn't let her play Pin-The-Tail-On-The-Donkey."

"Well, that wasn't what I said, but I thought it might have something to do with the game."

"I'll keep a close eye on her," Melissa promised, going quiet for a few seconds as she decided whether or not to tell him about their mother's vision regarding him. Melissa quickly decided to proceed, even though she knew he didn't put any stock in their mother's prophecies. "Mum had one about you, too. Did she happen to mention it?"

"She told me I would marry the girl at skating one day," he scoffed.

"Did she tell you about the accident?"

"No, she didn't mention an accident. Just that I would suffer some hardships before Candice and I tied the knot. I don't even know Candice that well Melissa, but it was strange that Mum knew about her. Do you think she travelled to Wotomba one day to spy on me?"

"Hardly," Melissa stated. "But she's been right before. Whether you believe in her or not, be careful."

"I always believe in Mum, Melissa. I just don't believe in her so-called visions. As for being careful, I always try to make the right decisions."

"Talk to you soon?"

"I'll stop in this afternoon on my way home. Enjoy the party, Liss."

"Enjoy skating. Maybe today will be the day you get to spend some time with Candice and get your future on track," she chuckled.

Cameron responded to that comment by ending the call.

He put his phone away and jumped on his bike. He would need to get a wriggle on, or they would leave without him.

The morning was muggy after the rain the day before. Sweat leaked from his pores and pooled beneath his armpits. Despite his lack of comfort, he pushed his body harder by pedalling faster. The warm breeze created by his movement didn't provide any relief. Luckily, he had packed his deodorant in his backpack the night before. He nearly didn't, expecting to be at the party instead.

He was dressed a little smarter than usual. He knew his friends would raise their eyebrows at his attire, but he had never really worried about getting their approval. His therapist had advised him to accept any offer of friendship extended to prevent him from disengaging from society. He was happy enough to hang out with them if they were willing to have him. If not, that was okay too. He would float until someone else offered their friendship, or not. The trick was to not let anyone get too close. That way, it wouldn't hurt so much when things went wrong.

He was the last to arrive at Adrian's and experienced a thread of fear when he laid his eyes on his friend's face. It appeared that Adrian's mood was somewhat reckless.

Five

Wearing dark coloured T-shirts with rude slogans plastered across the front in white, dark coloured cargo pants and white and dark grey joggers, Brad, Xavier and Tommy had their heads under the bonnet of a black, four door sedan, admiring the workings of the V8 engine, while Adrian gave it a rev. The sound from the exhaust was pure heaven to the boys, a symphony of possibilities. Knowing nothing at all about cars, Cameron couldn't tell what sort of car it was from where he stood, as he couldn't read the badging on the rear of the car but it looked like a late model.

"Hey Cameron. Listen to the sound of that V8 engine. Isn't she sweet?" commented Xavier.

"Does your dad know you're going to take it?" Tommy asked as Adrian got out of the driver's seat.

"Nope, but hey, if he is going to leave the spare set of keys lying around in the top drawer of his bedside table, who am I to say no to a test drive," Adrian replied.

"Isn't it illegal for people under the age of twenty-five and on a provisional licence to drive a high-performance vehicle?" Cameron questioned.

"Are you here to cause trouble?" Adrian snarled.

"No, I just thought I read in the road rules booklet that we weren't allowed to be in charge of a high-performance vehicle until we are on our open licence," Cameron replied.

"Dude, if you are going to be the fun police, maybe you should stay at home," Adrian suggested.

Cameron saw that his friends were becoming anxious. He didn't want to create an incident where they might have to divide their loyalties, so he tried to say something that would defuse the situation. "I'm cool, so are we taking her out?"

"Now you're talking," Tommy said, slapping Cameron on the shoulder blade. "Come on, Adrian, let's see what this puppy can do!"

The boys piled into the car. Adrian got behind the steering wheel with Tommy riding shotgun. They placed Cameron on the backseat in the middle so he wouldn't be tempted to open the door and exit the vehicle. Bradley sat behind Adrian and Xavier slid in behind Tommy. As soon as the doors were closed, Adrian put the car in gear and spun the wheels to the cheers of his passengers. A middle-aged woman passing by shook her head with disapproval.

Adrian drove towards the onramp to the highway leading to Wotomba. It was only an hour's drive from Dennings Hill and would allow them to see what speeds the car was capable of. There were too many intersections in the city to provide the engine with a good surge.

They hit the highway, and Adrian pressed the accelerator all the way to the floor. The speedo climbed swiftly, and the boys became flushed with adrenaline. It was the most excitement they had felt in their lives so far. Cameron did not even become upset as Bradley's, and Xavier's bodies slammed into him as Adrian weaved between the traffic.

While travelling up the Wotomba Range, the speed of the car dropped dramatically, almost coming to a crawl, due to large semi-trailers ahead of them having to drive in first gear. There was too much traffic coming in the opposite direction to risk overtaking across double lines. The boys felt they could walk faster than they were being forced to drive. Adrian took advantage of the couple of passing lanes when they were available but was still not happy about their progress.

Once they reached the summit of the range, however, the car picked up speed, and they flew along the highway once more. What should have taken an hour, took only forty minutes to achieve. Adrian had timed it perfectly and pulled into a parking space that was being vacated, right outside the bakery.

"Let's get something to eat," Adrian said. "I'm famished."

They scrambled out of the car and made their way inside. Pies, chips, and iced coffees were precisely what the boys needed. After placing their orders, they grabbed a table outside and set their numbers in the middle for the waitresses. Their eyes sparkled, and their cheeks were flushed from exhilaration.

"That was fantastic," Cameron enthused. "Adrian, how did you learn to drive like that?"

"Dude, I've been driving since I was thirteen. My uncle has a block of dirt in Glenvale and an old bomb that we thrash around in the paddocks. He's got all sorts of obstacles out there for us to hit or miss as we please."

"Who's we?" Xavier asked.

"Me and my brothers," Adrian answered.

"How many cars has he got out there?" Bradley asked.

"A few," Adrian hedged, not wanting them to invite themselves to a day of fun and frivolity at his special place.

"Here you go, boys," the waitress interrupted. "Now, who ordered the chicken and vegetable pies?" When Bradley and Cameron raised their fingers, she placed their order in front of them and asked, "Steak, bacon, and cheese?" After giving Tommy his meal, she said, "Then you two must have the steak, tomato, onion, and pepper pies," handing Adrian and Xavier their plates. "I hope you enjoy your food. Amy is coming with your drinks. Let us know if we can get you anything else."

The guys checked out her legs and rear end as she walked away, then began to eat their morning tea. Amy placed their iced coffees in front of them and left them to their meal.

"Nice staff around here," Bradley remarked.

"Yeah, nice," Tommy agreed. "What are you guys doing after graduation? I know Adrian is halfway through an apprenticeship in mechanics, and I'm looking into becoming an electrician."

"Brad and I are going into the family business."

"And what is that?" Cameron asked.

"Clowning," Xavier answered.

"What, like Ronald McDonald?"

"No, man, a rodeo clown. Like when a three hundred kilogram bull has thrown his rider off, and it is up to you, to stop it from goring him with his horns."

"Don't you have to be eighteen to do that?" Cameron queried.

"Nope, as long as the oldies give us permission by signing a form."

Seeing the look of disbelief displayed all over Cameron's face, Adrian decided to add a little more information. "I don't know about that, Cameron, but I do know that these two monkeys are turning eighteen in a couple of weeks. They were kept down in year one to learn how to interact with their peers. As twins, they tended to keep to themselves, and their teacher felt they needed some more socialising before moving on to the next year level."

"Yeah, stupid cow. I wonder what Mrs Gregory would think of our future aspirations?" Xavier asked.

"Dude, she will probably be the first woman to pay some money in the hopes of seeing you get gored," Adrian laughed. "What about you, Scholar? What are your future plans?" he asked Cameron. He hoped it was something that would require him to have to deal with a bunch of jokers like Xavier and Brad. They had no intentions whatsoever of becoming rodeo clowns. Their family business was law enforcement; dad was a cop and mum was a lawyer.

"I want to be a paramedic," Cameron answered.

"Figures," Adrian grunted.

"You can be such a downer sometimes, Adrian," Bradley said. "I think that is really cool, Cameron, and I wish you all the best with that."

"Yeah, man. That is an impressive career goal. Imagine all the people you could end up saving," Xavier encouraged.

"I could never do something like that," Tommy stated. "How could you consider working in a field where you are dealing with blood and guts, puke and poop, not to mention the drug and alcohol-fuelled violence that's been all over the news?"

"I want to help people," Cameron said with a shrug, eating the last of his pie.

"Let's go," Adrian said now that everyone had finished their meal.

"Thanks, it was awesome," Cameron told the waitresses as they left.

Adrian shook his head in annoyance. For some reason, he was more irritated than usual by Cameron's presence. He had been thinking seriously of leaving Cameron there to make his own way home, but, that would create an argument between the group. As he didn't feel like taking them all on, Adrian firmly suggested they get inside the car then drove them to the Wotomba Roller Skating Centre.

The building was two stories high. The lower level comprised of undercover parking while the upper level contained the skating rink, the food centre and a gaming room. It was constructed of concrete that was coated with a cream-based render. Not much to look at from the outside, it was only after stepping inside, that the pleasure meter increased. It was like being transported to another place.

The paintings on the walls had been commissioned by artists whose talents lay in bringing a canvas of the universe to life. Dazzling planets, comets, stars and the nebulae adorned the walls. The air conditioning unit was set to lower than standard to help create an atmosphere of vast emptiness between worlds. The joy of skating amongst the stars was so attractive it was difficult to step out into the world at the end of the session.

Cameron arrived at the counter, saddened to have some new guy serve him. He surveyed the Staff Only area of the facility, trying to catch sight of Candice.

"Where's Candice?" Adrian had asked the guy before Cameron had finished his surveillance.

"She's not working today."

"Since when does she have Saturdays off?"

"I guess, that would be since now," the attendant said with a sarcastic tone.

"Toby!" his boss cautioned.

"Are you getting the meal as well as the skates?" he asked Cameron, turning his attention back to him. Adrian scowled, annoyed that he was being made to go second.

"Yes, please."

Toby handed over the tickets for the skates and food then moved onto Adrian. Cameron walked to the shoe counter and placed his card on the tray.

"G'day mate, how you been?"

"Fine, Bert. How's about you?" Cameron answered.

"Can't complain. No-one will listen anyway," he replied. "I'm glad you came today. Candice was hoping you would come."

"Why is that?"

"She's liked you for a while, you know."

"No, I didn't know that."

"Yep, she likes you a lot, but she's always working, see." Cameron didn't see but waited for him to continue. "Now that she's got the day off, she was hoping you would come so she could spend some time getting to know you. Speak of the devil," he gazed off into the distance.

Cameron spun around to see Candice on the rink, skating in an anticlockwise direction. Her long ebony hair hung loosely, fluttering gently as she glided across the surface. She wore a pale blue figure skating outfit that had dark blue sparkles arranged in a rolling wave pattern. He watched her twirl, as fluid as a ballet dancer on her skates, then felt his pulse quicken as their eyes locked on each other.

'Holy moly, she's good,' he thought. Unlike him who, even when he had warmed up, couldn't skate in the reverse direction and had no clue how skating

backwards worked. Then he wondered what she thought of him on previous occasions as he clumsily made his way around the rink, but quickly decided he didn't want to know. Ignorance was bliss. Cameron broke the connection and moved to the closest booth to sit on the seat. He replaced his shoes with the skates and waited for the others to do the same.

Once they were all set, they rose to their feet and made their way to the rink. Stepping onto the slippery surface was always unsettling. Cameron wondered, as usual, if he was going to go bottoms up or not. Of all the days for that to happen, he was sure today would be the day. Luckily for him, he managed to stay on his feet by gripping the waist-high wall at the edges. He carefully made his way around the rink, getting used to the feeling of standing on wheels.

"Hello, Cameron," Candice murmured behind him.

Cameron turned to greet her and lost his balance. With his arms pin-wheeling to regain balance, he felt himself falling. Candice reached out to stop his fall, but he had gone too far and ended up taking her with him. The patron skating nearby jumped over them to avoid becoming a casualty himself.

Cameron groaned, not willing to admit that his pride hurt more than anything else. Candice lay on top of him, laughing with uncontrolled abandonment. She felt gentle fingers grab her under the arms and lift her to her feet. She spun around to find herself an arm's length away from Adrian's unamused face.

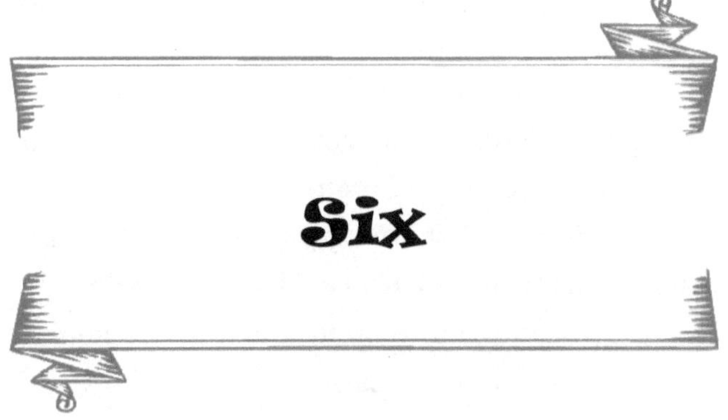

Six

Adrian grabbed her hand. Barely moving his feet, he glided away taking Candice with him. Once he'd put a few metres between Candice and Cameron, he stilled his feet and placed his hands on her waist.

"Did he hurt you?" he asked.

"No he didn't, and it was an accident," she said, placing her hands over his and flicking them off her body. Candice skated back to Cameron who had gotten to his feet and was hanging onto the wall to become accustomed to the feel of wheels on his feet. "Are you okay, Cameron?"

"Yeah, I'm fine. Sorry about that," he stuttered.

"Don't worry about it," she waved off his apology. "I practically live on these," she pointed to her skates. "You, not so much. Once you get your skating legs, you'll be whizzing around, wondering why you weren't able to do it sooner." He loved her smile. It made the world feel so much brighter. "Give me your hand."

Candice took him away from the safety of the edge, skating backwards so she could hold both his hands and keep an eye on his comfort level. He gripped her hands tightly at first, swinging them slightly as he learnt to maintain his balance. He wished he had been able to go skating more often. Then he wouldn't feel like such a baby. They passed Adrian, who had left the rink to sit at one of the tables. His glare was unsettling, to say the least. Candice also noticed. "What's his story?"

"I don't know. I figured you two must have dated."

"Nah, he's not my type."

"What is your type?"

"Oh, I don't know. Tall guys with shaggy brown hair, brown eyes, and an intelligent conversation or two up their sleeve."

Cameron looked around the rink in search of someone who fit that description. Candice flicked her wrist, which sent Cameron into a panic. His arms tried to pinwheel, but she held his hands firmly in hers. He leant forward and would have fallen over if she had not been robust enough to keep him steady. "What *are* you doing?"

"Trying not to fall," he grunted.

Candice was thankful she had asked for the day off. She had imagined Cameron to be a fun person to spend her time with, and he had proven her right. Even though he was out of his depth with the skating, and feeling vulnerable, he was willing to put himself out there to be with her. She loved the feeling of her hands nestled in his. Her colleague, Aaron, was in charge of the booth, and his voice rang clearly through the speakers, "Reverse direction."

"Sorry, Candice. That's me out."

"Don't be silly. We'll skate or fall together."

"But I can't skate this way," he shook his head.

"It's just a reversal of your foot movements."

"Nope, it's a matter of reaching inside my head and turning my brain around, for that to happen."

Candice snorted with laughter. Cameron decided he wanted to give her many opportunities to do that. Her eyes sparkled, and the sound of her enjoyment was intoxicating. She placed an arm around his waist. "We'll take it nice and slow." He wondered if she was talking about skating in the wrong direction or their friendship. He was too afraid to ask.

Cameron had never liked a girl before. There were girls he talked to at school, but not like Candice. She was special. He was afraid he would do something stupid, and she would lose interest in him. The feeling diminished as the minutes ticked by.

Candice spent the next half hour giving Cameron a private skating lesson. He thought that was funny, considering they were surrounded by over one hundred people. But by the end, he was able to skate semi-confidently in both directions and change directions without having to stop first. Candice seemed impressed, and Cameron was pleased to have been able to progress his skills with her help.

Now he just needed to work out how he was going to practise. He was still on his learner's permit. Before his test to get his P-plate licence, he needed to complete 100 hours of driving with a person who has an open licence sitting in the passenger seat. He didn't have the money to be able to afford more driving lessons per week. He couldn't ask his parents to take him more often as they already had commitments of their own, such as work and caring for Keeley so Melissa could study and increase her chances of securing a job with a decent income.

The speakers crackled to life and Aaron could be heard saying, "Could I have everyone off the floor." Skaters moved to their nearest exit and waited on the carpeted area for what was to come. "Speed skaters, take to the floor." Hoots of delight could be heard throughout the centre as a handful of skaters surged onto the surface of the rink, their feet performing an elegant dance across the surface. Their bodies rapidly outlining the perimeter of the arena in a couple of blinks of the eye.

They were getting into a groove when Aaron yelled, "Reverse direction." A loud scraping sound was heard above the beat of the music. They stopped swiftly then began skating in the other direction. Their feet crossing left over right as they rounded the corners. After another few minutes, Aaron called a halt to their session. Candice skated to the exit where Cameron waited and left the rink.

"You were amazing," his eyes sparkled with admiration.

"Thanks, Cameron. I need a drink."

She looped her arm through his. They skated across the carpet, a much more manageable feat than gliding on the slippery surface of the rink, then carefully climbed the stairs to the food bar. "What can I get you?" Bert asked cheerfully.

"My drinks are free, Cameron. Let me get you one." He didn't have any issues with Candice getting him a free drink and asked for a bottle of water. She asked for the same and pointed to his friends sitting in the same chairs they had used to put their skates on earlier. "Want to join them?"

"Sure, if you like."

Candice strode to the table, Cameron almost dawdled. He wasn't sure if he wanted to share her just yet and was a little afraid that she wouldn't like his friends. He needn't have worried. She had gauged their personalities over the weeks of serving them at the front counter and had watched the exchanges between them, on and off the rink. "Hey guys, looking good out there."

"Hi, Candice," Xavier glanced over his shoulder at Cameron, noticing the dejected look on his face. "Enjoying your day off?"

"Yeah, it's good to be able to get out on the floor with you guys. It's nice to not have to stand on the sidelines and watch you having fun and not being able to join in. I am enjoying mingling with you all."

"What you really mean," Bradley butted in, "is that you can play the games instead of running them, and can show us how much practice we still need to do to be in your league."

"Ha, good one, Brad," Tommy slapped his leg.

"That is not what I meant at all," she stated.

"No, of course not," Adrian grumbled, nodding his head towards Cameron. "You wanted to spend some time with lover boy there."

"What is your problem, Adrian?" Cameron asked.

"The only problem I have is when people don't say what they really mean. She requested the day off to spend time with you. End of story."

"Sounds like someone's jealous," Bradley said with a sing-song tone.

Adrian gave him the death stare, which made everybody feel uncomfortable. He pushed away from the group and entered the skating rink.

"Wow, he's pretty intense, isn't he?" Candice remarked.

"His feelings run deep. He's liked you for some time now," Xavier commented.

"I guess it might drive a wedge between you guys if I wanted to date Cameron?"

"You can't worry about that, Candice," Tommy said. "If you like Cameron, you have every right to go out with him. Adrian will just have to accept that you are not interested in him and move on."

"Easier said than done," Cameron grimaced, thinking about his mother's prophecy. According to her, Adrian was not going to be happy about Candice's choice. Perhaps he should find his own way home. She did mention something about an accident, and Adrian had *borrowed* his dad's beast of a car.

Cameron felt goosebumps break out on his skin. He was being stupid and scaring himself for no reason. The boys were there, they would keep Adrian in line. Besides, he didn't believe in his mother's mumbo-jumbo anyway. "Are you ready for more skating, or would you like to get something to eat?"

"More skating, I think. We still have an hour to go," she consulted her watch. "How about we eat in thirty minutes?" That was okay with Cameron. He could still feel the pie and iced coffee sitting in his stomach. Now that he'd found his balance, thirty minutes should be plenty of time to work up an appetite. Cameron and Candice skated hand in hand. For the second time within the last few months, he found himself feeling unsure of how he should react to a situation.

The first being the death of his brother-in-law. The second being in the presence of a person who was shaping up to be very important to his future. He was used to his head ruling all of his decisions. Now suddenly, his heart was guiding him into areas of mystery and intrigue.

Should he kiss her at the end of the session? Should he kiss her at the end of the song? Should he even be thinking about kissing her at all? How was he going to get himself to the rink more often? How often did Candice go there? Was she still at school?

Okay, he could get the answers to some of those questions while they consumed their meal. Others would require considerable risk on his part. He would take a chance that Candice would be gentle with him as he learnt how to behave in a relationship. If she gave him a sign that she wanted his affection, he would be more than happy to oblige. If it were too early for anything more than simple hand-holding, he would be pleased to wait, imagining what it would be like in the meantime.

He glanced over to catch her studying him. He felt warmth flooding his body and knew that his cheeks had turned a very bright red. He was saved from saying something utterly embarrassing when Aaron's voice crackled through the speakers.

"Righty-oh skaters, it is time to play a game. This one is called Red Rover. The rules are simple. Line up against the wall nearest my booth. My team will be out in the middle of the rink, ready to tag you. When you hear the whistle, skate to the opposite wall without being tagged, and you are still in play. Get tagged, and you will be required to exit the rink. Last skater standing wins a free session. On my mark."

The skaters had organised themselves during his spiel. Most of them were regulars and knew the drill. Cameron hadn't felt confident enough to remain on the floor and left by the nearest exit to watch Candice in action. He stood beside Brad, Tommy, and Xavier, who had also decided to give the game a miss.

The whistle blew, and he was enthralled by her grace. Her powerful legs pushed her quickly toward the middle. The team of blockers tried their hardest to tag her, but she was exceptional on her skates. She ducked beneath the first blocker's arm and jumped over the second's who had gone low. She reached the other side, touching the wall to indicate she was safe.

Candice turned around and waited for the next round. As soon as the rink was cleared of skaters racing to the other side or leaving due to being tagged, the whistle sounded again. Candice zoomed across the arena, touching the opposite wall in no time.

Cameron and his friends sent encouraging words Candice's way. After a few rounds, there were only a handful of people left out there. Candice was one as was Adrian.

The next round sounded, and the other three were prevented from reaching the safety of the wall, leaving Adrian and Candice as the remaining contenders. As Candice was a member of staff, Aaron announced that she was disqualified from the competition and awarded the prize to Adrian.

Candice skated over to Adrian. She held her hand out to congratulate him, but instead of shaking it, he used it to pull her forward and placed a kiss on her lips. Candice pushed him away and skated to the nearest exit.

Cameron moved to enter the rink but was stopped by Tommy. "Let it go, mate."

"I don't think so," he shook his head.

"Candice can handle this. She won't thank you for getting into a fight with Adrian."

"No, I know. But she won't think much of me if I don't stand up for her, either."

Candice had made a loop and stopped behind him. "I would think less of you if you were to lower yourself to his level. That was a cheap shot. I don't care much for people who steal what doesn't belong to them."

"What did he steal?" Xavier inquired.

"A kiss, Numbskull," his brother smacked him on the back of the head.

Candice linked her arm through Cameron's. "How about we get that meal?"

Adrian sulked in a corner, hating Cameron more than ever.

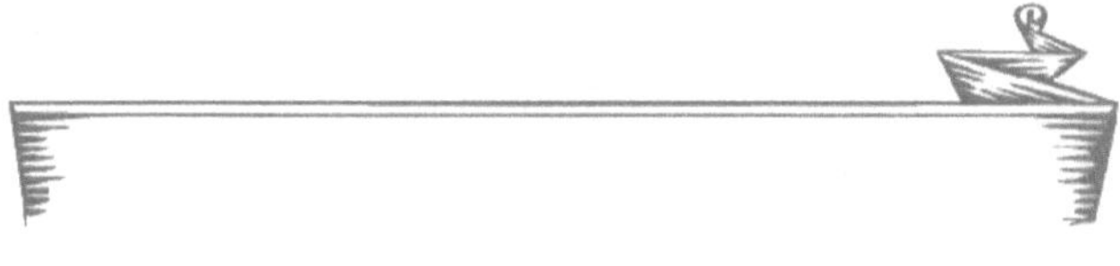

Seven

Cameron ordered a hamburger with a bucket of chips while Candice asked for a works hotdog with a side salad. He wiggled his eyebrows at her. "Do you think the salad outweighs the naughtiness of the added extras on the hotdog?"

"Not at all. But it is better than adding a whole load of calories from deep-fried chips to the mix."

"What will you have to drink?" asked Bert.

"I'll have a cola, please" Cameron replied before pointing to Candice.

"I'll have another bottle of water, please," she answered.

Cameron turned back with a lopsided smile, hoping to make up for his lack of manners by placing his order first. Bert had noticed his slip and was pleased to see that Cameron had realised as well. He let it go, giving them their number. This time, she chose to sit at a table for two rather than joining his friends. She didn't want to risk Adrian coming over to a seat and spoil their time together further.

"I'm sorry about Adrian," he began.

"Why? He's not your child and, even if he were, you are not responsible for the things that come out of his mouth, or his action for that matter."

"I still feel responsible. I did come with him, after all."

"I assume your other friends did as well?" He nodded his head in confirmation. "I don't see them coming over here to apologise. It's not their place, and it isn't yours. If anyone should be apologising, it's Adrian."

"Don't hold your breath."

"Oh, don't worry about him. I know what his type likes. He thinks it is me, but it's not. I'll bring my friend, Jala, with me next week. He will be utterly mesmerised by her and all of this will be forgotten."

They tucked into their food. The music thumped along with Candice's foot tapping in time. At one stage, a song with an unusually high bass came on, and Candice's leg overexerted itself, pushing her foot into Cameron's leg. "Oi," he said around a mouthful of food.

"Ooh, that is so gross," she squirmed. "Sorry for kicking you." Her leg stopped swinging as her body moved from side to side.

"Do you like to dance?" Cameron asked.

"Yes," she hedged, "but I am not as good at dancing as I am at skating."

"Great!" he beamed. "Would you like to go dancing with me next week?"

"Where abouts?"

"There is a dance studio a block away that has a room available in the afternoons."

"How do you know that?" she queried.

"My aunt owns the place and has been trying to get me to come and teach a hip-hop class for months."

"You hip-hop?" she gulped.

"Yep. So do you want to come? We don't have to hip-hop, but she has a pretty good sound system. We can waltz, tango, and dance the cha-cha or the mambo." Dropping his voice to a whisper and placing his hand to the side of his mouth, he said, "We could even decide to be brave like superheroes and just do our own thing." Raising his voice and dropping his hand, he continued, "It will be loads of fun, and there'll be nobody there to laugh at us for being silly."

"Are you going to skate in the morning?"

"I have committed to taking care of my niece in the morning. She is only three and too young to come with me."

"We have Kinder Club that starts at seven. I am sure she would love it, and you would be amazed at how quickly they pick it up."

"My sister won't have time to drive us here and get back for her exam," he sighed. "It's okay if you don't want to dance with me."

His invitation sounded fun, but she wasn't sure if she was ready to trust him being alone with her. She hardly knew the guy. He was fun to be with, and she enjoyed holding his hand, but that was as far as she wanted their relationship to go for now. "I'm not sure what my roster is for next weekend yet. It won't get posted until tomorrow, and I don't want to ask for another day off so soon," she sighed.

"That's okay, we can work it out later. I don't even know how I am getting here next week. Adrian probably won't let me in his car after today, and I will have to ask my sister if she would be able to drive me up here after her exam."

"You could always catch the bus. Oh, wait, it only travels first thing in the morning and last thing in the afternoon. Guess that's not a valid option."

Cameron placed the last of his chips in his mouth and picked up their rubbish. He stood then walked the few steps to the bin, and put the wrappings inside. *Pity I don't have my licence yet,'* he thought.

Aaron's voice blasted through the speakers. "Skaters, can you please clear the floor for our couple skaters. Lovebirds, this set is for you."

As soon as the first track began to play, the lights dimmed to a romantic glow. Various positions were taken up as couples made their way onto the rink. Some held hands, while others simply glided side by side. A few of them chose to skate one behind the other, remaining tethered with gentle fingers to the waist of the one in front. A few couples decided to face one another, the more confident of the two skating backwards.

Cameron wondered how the last lot didn't end up with their feet tangled together. Candice led him onto the rink to join in with the other duos. A spotlight moved across the floor in random sweeps, highlighting pairs for a second before seeking out a new set. They skated side by side as they slowly made their way around the perimeter.

It seemed like no time had passed before Aaron was calling for all skaters to re-enter the rink. "Ten minutes remaining Skaters before the session ends. We would like to thank you all for coming and remind you to return any hired skates to the counter before leaving the premises. The next session begins in an hour. If you wish to attend that session, you will need to exit the centre and re-enter when the doors open fifteen minutes before the commencement time.

Travel home safely, and we hope to see you all again real soon."

The music came to an end, and the harsh fluorescent lights brightened the room. People left the rink and began replacing their skates for shoes. Cameron and Candice took their time preparing to go, stretching it out as far as they could. "What are you doing for the rest of the day?" he asked.

"I'm going to hang around for the next session. I have a figure skating class after that. It seems pointless to go home and then come back again."

"How far away do you live?"

"An hour."

Cameron felt himself getting excited. He lived an hour away, too. "Where do you live, Candice?" he asked with heart in mouth.

"Coobarra Falls. Why, where do you live?"

His heart fell. She lived an hour in the opposite direction to his place. "Dennings Hill," he answered. He noticed the disappointment cross her face and knew that she had also realised they lived two hours apart from one another. "Do you have video chat?"

"Yes."

"Maybe we could video chat each other?"

"That would be great," he smiled, spirits lifted. Cameron handed Candice his phone, "Call yourself."

Her body stiffened in response to his demand. "Please," he softened his tone and looked at her with puppy dog eyes. "Then I will have your number, and you will have mine." She couldn't stop a smile from spreading across her face as she typed in the numbers and pressed the dial icon. A smirk appeared on Cameron's face as her pocket began ringing. Candice ended the call, and Cameron saw movement in his peripheral vision. He glanced over to see Brad and Tommy moving their weight from one leg to another.

Realising the boys were getting restless, he gave her a quick kiss on the cheek before making his way to the exit. Adrian was in a foul mood when he reached the car. Cameron thought about not getting in with him but decided not to be such a baby. Surely, Adrian wouldn't do anything to put their lives at risk. Of course, he didn't allow his brain to linger on their drive there and the speeds Adrian was doing at the time. Adrian had been in a good mood then, and even though they were speeding, he had still felt safe.

Cameron jumped in the back seat, moving across until he was in the middle and put his seat belt on. The boys hopped in either side and buckled up, too. With a rev of the engine, Adrian drove thirty kilometres above the speed limit in the car park, nearly wiping out a few pedestrians.

Candice watched them from the top of the stairs with trepidation in her heart. She sent Cameron a quick text. **Let me no when ur home safe.** Cameron posted a reply. **Will do.**

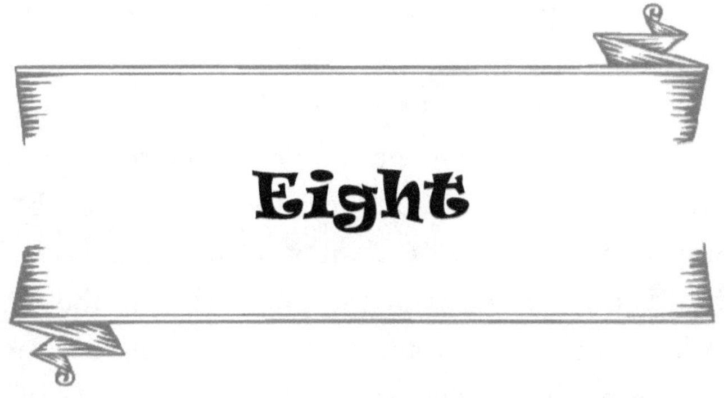

Eight

Adrian pushed the car further than he had before. Anger rolled off him in waves making everybody very uncomfortable. No-one spoke. Not even Tommy, who usually kept Adrian highly amused with one anecdote after another. The silence became unbearable, to the point where halfway home, Tommy decided to break it.

"So, are you taking us home or somewhere else?"

Adrian shifted his head in Cameron's direction, "I'm taking him home. I haven't decided what to do with you traitors yet."

"Traitors? What the hell are you talking about?" Tommy spluttered.

"I know you're all on *his* side. Candice was supposed to be my girl, not his."

Cameron opened his mouth to say something and copped an elbow in the ribs from both sides. Instead of words spewing from his lips, a grunt escaped instead.

"Shut it," Xavier whispered to him.

"That's not up to either of you to decide," Tommy said, getting a kick to his seat for his troubles. Brad was attempting to stop Tommy from talking as well, but Tommy was not in the mood to take the hint. Adrian's undeserved anger was getting his back up, too. "Candice is the only one capable of deciding who she wants to date. Not you, and not him."

Adrian's rage deepened. His foot pressed the accelerator further, and the car responded accordingly. It was becoming harder to judge how quickly they were approaching the vehicles in front of them, and their lane changes had become quite erratic. Calls were made to the police by passengers in other cars using the highway. Pretty soon, sirens were heard coming their way.

Adrian panicked. He glanced in his mirrors, not bothering to keep an eye on what was happening in front of him. Tommy shouted instructions, then gripped the wheel and yanked hard to the left, causing the car to veer suddenly. They narrowly avoided hitting a vehicle in front of them.

"Keep your eyes on the road!" Tommy's frightened voice bellowed. Adrian's eyes returned to the windscreen. He continued to weave between the other vehicles on the road. Then he spotted the police cars.

There were three of them, travelling in the opposite direction. Adrian grinned and gunned the accelerator further, his foot fully depressed to the floor by this stage. The boys started praying to every god they could name and then to some they couldn't.

The police cars crossed the grassed divide, matching him in a high-speed dance, allowing him to keep the lead, for now. They ordered Adrian to pull over, but he ignored their pleas. He was not going to lose points off his licence and maybe end up with a criminal record.

The exit from the highway came up fast, and he nearly missed it. The police following him did, but by then the police helicopter had arrived. It was following Adrian's car from the air and coordinating the other police cars that had joined the action into a safe place where the spike strip, a device used to puncture tyres, could be deployed.

Adrian didn't hear the blades of the chopper. He saw its shadow move across their path on the bitumen. "That's a damned helicopter, isn't it?"

"Yes, Adrian," Tommy replied. "You need to pull over."

"Don't be daft. We just need to take the next exit and find somewhere to dump the car. Dad will discover it missing eventually and report it stolen. Wipe down anywhere you might have touched. They will expect to find my fingerprints in here, but not yours."

The boys weren't able to do as he asked without taking their seatbelts off and removing their shirts, which they weren't about to do. When asked if they had completed the tasks, they all agreed the car was clean. Only Tommy, who was in the front seat with access to the last tissue in the glove compartment, was able to attempt the task safely. He had no idea whether his prints had been removed or not. He figured for the wipe-down process to be effective, the surfaces would need to be sprayed with something capable of lifting his skin's oily residue.

Tommy continued pleading with Adrian to stop. Adrian turned to Tommy to tell him to shut up when their car ran a stop sign and collided with another. The sound of the cars being ripped apart was horrendous. Residents who were home thought a bomb had gone off in their area. The cars spun out of control, each ending up in the front yards of two different residences.

Had it happened during peak time, the carnage would have been far higher. As it was, only the two cars were involved. The nearest police car was minutes away, and the policemen in the helicopter were in contact with emergency services. Ambulance officers and the Fire Brigade were on the way to offer assistance.

Cameron stood in the middle of the street. He was dazed and unable to comprehend the situation. The car they had been travelling in was barely recognisable. The metal twisted in ways that no human would ever have been able to accomplish. The force must have been tremendous.

The front of the vehicle no longer existed. The bumper bar, front grille, bonnet and everything beneath had been pushed into the area where Adrian and Tommy had been sitting. The side of the car where Xavier sat, had been crumpled like a piece of paper. Long tendrils of smoke drifted from the car, indicating the possibility of a fiery explosion.

His attention turned to the other car. It was a small blue hatchback which had come out in even worse shape. From what he could see, there seemed to be only one occupant in the vehicle. Scrutinising the scene before him, he was pretty sure there could be no survivors. Yet, he couldn't bring himself to check. People came running from nearby homes, and

Cameron was happy to leave the heroics to all of them. The last thing he wanted was to have the images of the victims haunt him forever, too.

As his eyes continued to move, registering the scene before him, he spotted Adrian and Tommy a hundred or so metres down the road. Adrian was viewing the chaos he had created through his reckless actions. Cameron watched them talking with one another, gesturing wildly. He frowned. *'Why are those two here?'* he wondered. The police vehicles arrived at the scene, causing Adrian to panic.

He took off with Tommy in quick pursuit. They hadn't gone far when Cameron noticed a man in a business suit appear before them. The boys thinking he was a policeman, slid to a stop and tried to reverse direction. The man placed his hands on their shoulders, and the three of them disappeared.

"What the hell?" Cameron blurted out fearfully.

He looked around but couldn't see them anywhere. An ambulance screeched to a stop with the driver and passenger exiting the vehicle quickly. The driver went to the car that Adrian had been in while the passenger raced to the other vehicle. Cameron wracked his brains to discover how he had come to be standing in the middle of the intersection but could not find any answers to his question. He didn't remember leaving the car.

He was terrified. An alien had just stolen his friends, and he was the only one aware that it had happened. Everyone else had been too busy focussing on the accident.

Cameron walked over to one of the police officers and tried to get his attention. Just like everyone else, he was too busy concerning himself with the injured. Cameron looked around and realised it was probably not safe to stay there. If the alien came back and took him too, would anyone be the wiser?

Why had he come there in the first place? He couldn't remember how he'd gotten there. He didn't even know where he was. Cameron did another sweep of the area, this time taking note of the landscape. The location seemed familiar, calming his panic slightly.

"Camwon," a familiar voice called to him.

Within seconds of the accident occurring, Carly, the owner of one of the houses, hurried down the stairs to assess the situation. Phone in hand, she was already in contact with the emergency call centre. She hoped her friend Melissa, who was studying to become a nurse and lived on the opposite corner of the intersection, was home and able to offer assistance. But when she peered inside the vehicle on her front lawn, she began to sob, *"No, no, no, no."*

"Carly!" Melissa shouted from the fence line.

"Don't come over, Melissa. Stay and take care of Keeley."

"She'll be fine," Melissa yelled, closing the gate behind her.

"No, I got it. The paramedics will be here in two minutes. Stay with Keeley."

"How about you go and look after Keeley, and I'll take care of the injured. This is what I will be doing for a living," Melissa reached the boot of the vehicle, finding her path blocked by Carly.

"Please, Melissa," Carly said with tears in her eyes.

"Get out of the way!"

"Cameron's in the car. I think he's dead," Carly sobbed.

"What do you mean he's dead?" Melissa asked, pushing Carly out of the way to see for herself. She tried to open the door, but it was stuck. "You haven't even checked his vitals," Melissa growled at her.

"Melissa, stop. The door is jammed, we need to try the other side."

Melissa and Carly ran around the back of the vehicle and began pulling on the handles to the door on that side. The door opened after a couple of tries. Melissa placed her fingers against the carotid artery of the nearest boy and found a faint pulse. Next, she leant across to the middle to check on that passenger, realising it was Cameron. A pole had come through the windscreen, piercing his chest close to where his heart was located. His head lolled to the side. Blood ran from his mouth where a few of his teeth were missing and continued down his chin where it dripped onto his shirt.

"God, Cameron," Melissa howled.

Carly dragged Melissa out of the car and hugged her fiercely. "I'm so sorry, Melissa. I didn't want you to see him like this. Go home and take care of Keeley. I will stay and assist the police and the ambulance when it arrives. As soon as they come and I tell them what I know, I will come and help you, okay?"

Melissa just stared at her. All she could see was the vision of Cameron. Carly walked her friend across the road, told her to stay with Keeley, then hurried across the street to see if anyone in the other vehicle had a pulse. Melissa barely registered the arrival of the police.

Cameron spun around and recognised the house on the corner. It belonged to his sister, Melissa. He walked to the fence and peered over the pickets. His niece Keeley was sitting in her front yard and had been peering through the gaps. She grinned up at him, her blonde hair hanging loosely and her blue eyes sparkling with happiness to see him. "Hello, Camwon."

"Hello, Keeley. How are you?" he asked.

"Good. Where you come fwom?" she rose to her feet.

"I'm not sure, I think my friends dropped me off," he answered. "How was the party?" he bent down to her eye level.

"It was weally good," she jumped up and down excitedly.

"Keeley, come over here, baby," her mother opened the gate.

"Why?" Keeley asked.

"Because, I need you to," Melissa sniffled.

"You come, too," Keeley told him firmly, reaching up to grab his hand.

"Now, Keeley," Melissa said a little firmer, walking towards her.

"I come, Mamma," Keeley dropped her hand and ran to Melissa who scooped her up in her arms.

"We need to go inside now," Melissa said.

"You sad, Mamma?" Keeley wiped the tears from her mother's cheeks.

"Yeah, baby. Mamma sad."

"You sad, too, Camwon?" Keeley twisted in her mother's arms to see him.

"No, Keeley, I'm not sad," he frowned. "Melissa, what's wrong?"

"Cameron's not here darling," her voice hitched. Cameron attempted to place his hand on Melissa's shoulder, but it passed straight through, causing her to shiver.

"He there," Keeley pointed to him.

"Okay, sweetheart. I am going to take you inside now. How about you ask Uncle Cameron to come with you and keep you company while I take care of some business. Carly, from across the street, is going to come and stay with you for a little while, okay?"

"Hmmm," Keeley nodded. "Come, Camwon," Keeley said as Melissa's tears flowed harder and she carried her daughter inside the house. Keeley quite often 'played' with Cameron when he wasn't there. Of all the days for Keeley to pretend that Cameron had come for a visit.

Keeley was placed on the floor in the lounge room. Melissa ventured into the kitchen where she washed her hands then quartered a small apple after carefully eliminating the skin and seeds. She placed the pieces in a bowl and handed it to her daughter.

"There you go, Pumpkin. Eat up." Melissa filled her Sippy cup with water and placed it on the coffee table beside her. Keeley shoved an entire piece of apple in her mouth and tried to chew. Melissa reprimanded her for stuffing her face, then realised it was her fault for not cutting the pieces small enough. Melissa grabbed the apple from Keeley's mouth and threw it in the bin, then picked up the bowl and cut the remaining pieces into thirds. "There you go, Pumpkin. That's better, isn't it? Silly Mummy." Keeley shoved another bit in her mouth and nodded her head.

Melissa knew she had to get a hold of her parents before they found out from someone else, but she didn't know how to go about telling them their son had died. She thought about the different ways she could begin the discussion when she saw them, but none of them seemed adequate.

She wanted to get it sorted before she hopped in her car because the last thing her parents needed was to have her become involved in an accident herself. Carly arrived within half an hour to take care of Keeley while Melissa spoke to her parents. Melissa still hadn't worked out what to say.

"What am I going to tell them?" she wailed.

"Love, they are going to know as soon as they see you that something is wrong. Walk inside, give them a big hug, and tell them the facts as gently as you can," Carly soothed. "They have taken Cameron to hospital in an ambulance."

"Maybe I should take Keeley with me. They might find some comfort in her."

"You could be right about that. It is your choice. I am happy to look after her for as long as you need me to."

"Thanks, Carly, but I might take her with me."

"Will you be home for dinner?"

"Probably."

"Come on over. I will cook extra and heat it up if it is late when you get here."

Melissa gave Carly a hug and then quickly gathered up some stuff in a bag for Keeley. "Come on, Pumpkin, we are going to Grandma's house."

"Can Camwon come?"

"No, baby."

"You can't come with us, Camwon. Mamma won't let you. You come back tomorrow to play?"

"Yes, Keeley, I will come back tomorrow to play," his hand ruffled through her hair, without putting a strand out of place.

Cameron walked outside and viewed the scene. The cars were being placed on tow trucks, and the ambulances had gone. The police vehicles were still on site while the officers collected evidence. The firefighters were busy cleaning up spilt petrol and removing the twisted shards of metal that had been ripped off the vehicles when they'd collided.

Cameron closed his eyes and tried to remember what he had been doing. He recalled standing around the car, admiring the sound of the engine and the sleek lines of the bodywork. Adrian had the keys. It must have been his car. Tommy was throwing his hands around excitedly, but Cameron couldn't make out what he was saying. Brad and Xavier had their heads under the bonnet and he, as usual, was slightly off to the side, not really a part of the group.

They must have gone for a drive in the car because the car hadn't been outside his sister's place when they first saw it. The next thing he recalled was standing in the middle of the road looking at Adrian and Tommy, who were located further along. Then the man in the suit had arrived, and all three of them had disappeared.

Cameron opened his eyes and searched the area but couldn't find them. He wondered where Xavier and Brad had ended up and discovered he was standing at the bottom of Brad's bed, in an emergency room cubicle. He looked dreadful.

His eyes were bruised and swollen, and his nose was clearly broken, no longer sitting straight down the middle of his face. His face was caked with blood, and three of his teeth were poking through the skin of his chin. His right shoulder was lopsided, and his breathing was shallow. Tubes were coming off him everywhere, and the room buzzed with the sounds of the machinery keeping him alive.

Cameron wandered out of the room, passing straight through the door without realising it had been closed. His mind was in turmoil as he came to understand they must have been in an accident, and he was probably dead and unable to return to the living. He ached for his mother. She always managed to make him feel as though everything was going to be okay. Before he knew it, he was standing in her living room.

She was seated beside his father at the round, wooden breakfast table. A handkerchief perched in her hand was pressed tightly against her mouth.

Keeley sat on her Grandfather's lap while Melissa sat opposite them both, holding one of their hands in each of her own. His mother's honey-coloured hair was up in a French knot, and the mascara that helped her eyelashes appear longer and fuller streaked down her cheeks. The blue eyeshadow she preferred to wear was smudged, and her eyes were closed as she attempted to digest the news.

His father was a wretched sight. Cameron had only ever witnessed him cry once before, and it was absolutely heart wrenching. He appeared broken, miserable. Nothing like the funny, cheerfully good-natured bloke who had instilled in Cameron the confidence to try new things. It was his father who had nurtured his belief that he could become whatever his heart desired.

Cameron felt a stabbing pain in his chest. He had thrown his life away by trying to fit in with guys that he didn't really have anything in common and one especially that he had no respect for, so that he might appear less nerdy to the girls. Instead of standing on his own two feet and being taken on his own merits, he had let his father down by making the wrong choices.

Keeley had been playing with a pen that lay on the tablecloth and looked up at that moment to find Cameron standing despondently before her. "Camwon," she cried, holding her arms out to him to be picked up.

"Keeley, stop it!" Melissa barked at her.

Keeley burst into tears while Cameron tried to calm her. "Don't cry, Keeley. Mummy, Grandmother and Grandfather, can't see me. I am magic and have become invisible. Only you can see me. Sh," he placed his finger over his lips. Keeley stopped crying and watched him.

"Can you see Uncle Cameron, Keeley?" Grandmother asked. Cameron shook his head from side to side, and Keeley copied. "Are you sure?" Cameron nodded his head up and down while Keeley followed suit.

"What are you doing, Mother?" Melissa questioned.

"I wondered if Keeley had been blessed with the gift of conversing with the dead," she replied.

"How would that be a gift? It's more like a curse if you ask me."

"Well, nobody is asking you!" her mother snapped. "Your great-grandmother had the gift, and she helped many lost souls cross over into the next life."

"If there is a next life, I am sure Cameron is already there. What would he hang around for?" Melissa retorted.

"Unfinished business. Maybe he doesn't know he is dead and needs to be told it is okay to go into the light."

"Will you listen to yourself?" Melissa barked furiously getting to her feet. "Dad, say something!"

"There is nothing to say. I don't know what happens after somebody dies. I have never done it myself. Maybe Keeley can see him, maybe she can't. Who's to know but Keeley herself, and she says she doesn't. You will believe what you believe, your mother will believe what she believes. The only thing I believe is that a child should not die before their parents, and I will have to live out the rest of my days without my son." He placed Keeley on the floor then pushed his wiry frame away from the table, standing on unsteady feet. He wiped the tears from his bloodshot eyes, then wiped his hand on his white singlet as he left the room.

"Look at what you've done!" Melissa's mother bawled.

"What I've done!" Melissa took a few deep breaths and stood perfectly still. "We are both upset and suffering from a significant loss. I am going to take Keeley home before we say something we can't take back. Call me when you are ready. I love you, Mum."

Melissa took Keeley by the hand and led her to the door. As she opened it, she heard her mother say, "I love you, too." Melissa closed the door and got Keeley settled in the car. She listened to the shrill of the house phone and decided it was somebody letting her parents know of Cameron's death. "Couldn't even do it in person," she muttered.

With an angry heart, Melissa drove them home. It was a bit early, but she stopped in at Carly's for dinner, anyway. Goodness knew she needed the company.

Ten

It was nearly dark. Cameron wasn't sure where he was. Time and space seemed to work differently now, which helped to keep him confused. He didn't recognise the room he stood in.

It reminded him of Keeley's room, but everything was washed out and grey. The curtains covering the windows should have been pink. The wallpaper used to be cream with white unicorns, pink flowers, and brightly coloured rainbows. A single bed which was perched in the middle of the far wall had a pillowcase and bedspread covered in pictures of greyed out fairies.

A wooden toy box with a picture of a fairy sitting upon a unicorn ran alongside another wall. Cameron sat on the lid and tried to shake his confusion. He figured a person would come along sooner or later that might shed some light on his location. He never expected it to be the man in the suit.

The guy stood quietly, appraising Cameron's appearance. Cameron took the opportunity to do the same; the man was a stocky Asian with black hair and brown eyes. The head of a red dragon tattoo poked out the top of his white collared shirt. His pants and jacket were navy blue as were his shoes.

"Where did you come from?" Cameron asked him.

"Nowhere, everywhere," the man responded with a deep timbered voice.

"That tells me nothing," Cameron mumbled. "Who are you?"

"Wang Cho."

"Did you hurt my friends?"

"No. I do not hurt people, I help them move on."

"To where?"

"The next part of their journey, though I do not enter the next realm."

"Why not?"

"It is not part of my destiny. I am the guide between this realm and the next."

"You're a Reaper?"

"Yes."

"So, I'm dead?"

"No, you are not. *You* are in limbo."

"Limbo? What does that mean?"

"You are between the living and the dead."

"Are you waiting for me to die?"

"You are not on my list, Cameron, but if you do not return to your body, you soon will be. I am giving you a chance to save yourself."

"How do I do that?"

The door to the bedroom slammed against the wall giving Cameron a fright.

Wang took hold of Cameron's arm, holding him to the ghostly plane.

"Get your pyjamas, Keeley, while I run your bath," Melissa's voice carried through the hallway.

Keeley entered the room, giggling with happiness. She quickly moved to her bed and deftly climbed on top of the mattress. Lifting up her pillow, she exposed her pyjamas hidden beneath. She pulled them towards her and dropped the pillow. Holding them in her hand, she slid off the bed and scurried to the bathroom. Cameron's smiling eyes turned to face Wang, but he had gone.

Cameron had no idea how to save himself. He didn't even know where to find his body. No matter how hard he tried to will himself back into his body, his spirit remained in Keeley's room. He didn't want to watch Keeley have her bath, so he pottered around in her room.

There was nothing to look at, not even a photo. Melissa didn't believe in things lying around, messing up the place. Keeley had to put everything away when she was finished playing with it. The only thing of Keeley's he could see in the room was Horsey, her tan coloured rocking horse. He then realised that the colours had returned.

Cameron attempted to lift the lid of her toy box, but his hands were unable to grip the wood and passed through. He tried again with the same result. Cameron wandered over to Keeley's bed hoping to turn down the sheets, but he was not able to move them, either.

Growling in frustration, he stamped his foot and found himself passing through the floorboards. Panic set in, and he managed to raise himself but overshot the mark. Cameron hovered half a metre above the floor with his head rubbing the ceiling. "Oh, come on!" he yelled into the atmosphere.

"Ahhh," Keeley sucked in her breath while in the bathtub. She looked at Melissa with eager eyes and said, "Uncle Camwon's here."

"Oh, Keeley, I wish you would give it a rest."

"Hurry, Mamma, I get out," she said, getting to her feet and raising her arms to be lifted out.

Melissa said, "Sit down, Keeley, you still have shampoo in your hair."

Keeley sat down with a frown. She was eager to see Cameron and play with him. Melissa grabbed a round plastic container and filled it with the bathwater. "Close your eyes, baby," she said as she poured it over Keeley's head.

The shampoo ran down Keeley's face and neck while she blew air, making bubbling sounds. Melissa repeated the process a couple more times before wiping the water from Keeley's eyes. "Boo," she said, to Keeley's delight.

Keeley raised her arms again, and this time Melissa lifted her out. She wrapped Keeley in a towel and pulled the plug. When Melissa turned around to dry her, she was gone. "Keeley?"

No answer. Melissa followed the wet footsteps to Keeley's room and found her sitting in the far corner of the room, talking to herself. Keeley was staring at the wall in front of her while her hands flapped excitedly as though trying to fly. "I didn't know you could do that," Keeley giggled.

"Keeley, you've got water all over the floor. Come here. You need to get dry and put your PJs on."

"You stay?" she asked Cameron.

"Yep."

Keeley stood up and ran to the bathroom. She allowed Melissa to do what was required now that she knew Cameron wasn't going to leave. Keely was in her element. Playtime with Uncle Cameron was just like it was when he actually came for a visit. Except it felt different when she cuddled him. There was no warmth nor substance to him anymore. It still sounded the same when he talked to her, though.

After Melissa had dressed her, then brushed her hair and teeth, they wandered back to her bedroom. Melissa asked Keeley to hop into bed. Keeley went to argue with her Mum, but Cameron said, "Jump up, Keeley."

Melissa watched as her daughter complied with her request without argument and felt a bit uneasy. She knew Keeley wasn't tired, even though Melissa was exhausted, and needed some rest. "Do you want me to stay with you?" she asked.

"No, Mamma. I good."

Melissa tucked her in and kissed her on the forehead. "Good night, Pumpkin. Love you forever."

"Good night, Mamma. Love you fowever, too."

Melissa turned the night lamp on, a small plastic figure shaped like a lamb that held a light bulb inside its tummy, then turned off the ceiling light. Melissa left the door ajar and walked to the bathroom for a shower. Cameron watched her go and thought he should follow her. Although she was not a fully qualified nurse, she knew more about the workings of the human body than he did, Cameron mused.

Perhaps she would be able to give him some ideas on how to return his soul to his body. He wanted to follow her to attempt communication again, but Keeley had other plans. She wanted him to tell her a story. As he was about to begin, the phone in the hallway started ringing.

"Hang on, Keeley, I've just got to answer the phone."

"Mamma get it," Keeley tapped her hand on the blanket for Cameron to sit with her.

He glanced at the door then said, "Okay, what do you want to hear tonight?"

"The Pwincess and the Unicorn," Keeley squealed.

Cameron settled in beside her and began telling the story.

A long time ago, in a faraway land lived King David, Queen Melissa, and their daughter, Princess Keeley. They were dearly loved by their people because they were kind and gave them lots of goodies to eat.

"Like what?" Keeley asked.

"Like cupcakes, chocolate, and fairy floss," Cameron smiled.

One day, while walking through the streets of their kingdom with baskets of goodies, a woman approached them and asked them for some fruit. King David and Queen Melissa looked at one another, shocked that the woman would ask for something so strange.

"Why are apples strange?" Keeley asked.

"King David and Queen Melissa thought apples were boring food. They thought their people would be happier being given sweet treats rather than food that is good for them to grow up big and strong," Cameron replied.

"Why would you ask for such a thing?" Queen Melissa asked the woman.

"While the cakes, chocolate, and floss are yummy, Your Majesty, our teeth are beginning to blacken and hurt," the woman said.

King David and Queen Melissa looked at the woman's smile then pulled back in fright at the state of her mouth. Her teeth were indeed turning black, and pieces of some teeth were missing altogether.

"Can they be fixed, Uncle Camwon?"

"Sh, wait and see," he placed his hands on her cheeks.

King David and Queen Melissa took a deep breath and looked very sad. "This is terrible," King David said to the woman. "We only wanted to make you happy."

"I know that, Your Majesty. I would like to have an apple if you have one to spare," the woman said.

"Mamma gives me apple every day," Keeley told Cameron.

"I know. They are good for your body, Keeley."

"The Unicorn help?"

"Let's find out."

King David and Queen Melissa asked the woman to trek to the castle to ask the grounds people to pick the biggest, juiciest apples for her and her family to eat. Then they talked to one another to find an answer to the problem their people faced.

How could they continue to give their people sweet foods without hurting their teeth? King David and Queen Melissa were stuck. They didn't know what to do, but Princess Keeley did.

"We should go and see the Unicorn. He is most wise," Princess Keeley said.

King David and Queen Melissa hugged their daughter. "As are you," the Queen replied.

"Yay. We go to see the Unicorn," Keeley cried.

Melissa opened the door, walked into the room then proceeded to sit on top of Cameron. "Keeley, I need to tell you something," she began.

"Okay, what is it Mamma," some of the sparkle left Keeley's eyes.

"Uncle Cameron is very sick and is in a big white building called a hospital, with other very sick people. We are going to go and sit with him, but you need to be very quiet and very still. Can you do that, Pumpkin?"

Keeley was confused. Cameron had been sitting right beneath her mother but had managed to drag himself out and was standing by her shoulder. She frowned at Melissa, causing her mother to sigh. "I'll see if Carly can come over and watch you. I'll try to be home before you wake up in the morning," she said, getting to her feet.

"I'll come," Keeley raised her arms.

Melissa picked up her daughter and placed her feet on the floor. She retrieved a pair of slippers from beneath the bed and a dressing gown from the cupboard. They hurried to the car then made their way to the hospital.

Melissa knew they wouldn't allow Keeley inside the Intensive Care Unit. She also knew without Keeley's presence, her parents might refuse to forgo some time with Cameron so that she could sit with him for a while.

Eleven

Cameron had more colour in his cheeks than when Melissa had seen him last. The pole had been removed from his chest, and he had been placed in a chemically induced coma. The room was resonating with the hissing of a ventilator and the beeping of a heart monitor as the blip moved across the screen.

Melissa stood on the opposite side of the bed to her mother. She would have preferred her father to be in the room with her, but he had insisted on staying in the waiting room with Keeley. The women gently stroked Cameron's hands as they waited patiently for a sign he had registered their presence. Cameron's eyes remained closed, and his hands stayed limp.

The temperature of the room was a comfortable twenty-four degrees, but the atmosphere felt much cooler than that. Words that had passed between them earlier still hung in the air. Neither willing to break the ice and make amends.

While Cameron was unable to feel the emotional rift between his favourite girls, their behaviour brought a frown to his face. He wondered if there was something else on the table besides him lying unconscious that was causing animosity between them.

"Come on, Cameron. Wake up," Melissa encouraged, leaning in and brushing the hair off his forehead.

"He'll wake up when he's ready," her mother stated more tersely than she had meant to.

Melissa was unable to hold her tongue, "Did you see *that* in your vision, too?"

"What are you more upset about, Melissa? The fact that I knew the accident was going to happen or that I couldn't see enough to prevent it from happening?"

Melissa refused to be baited by her mother. To answer that question, Melissa would have to admit she was terrified that the vision that Keeley starred in would come true. She gently brushed his forehead with her thumb, "Come back to us, Cameron. Keeley needs her uncle, as do I."

Cameron could feel himself being pulled towards his body. He started to feel excited. Melissa was helping his soul become reconnected to his body. A feat he hadn't known how to accomplish himself.

His spirit travelled to the end of his bed then slowly rose into the air. His position changed from upright to horizontal. Cameron slowly hovered over his body, getting ready to settle inside when his mother's terrified moans broke the euphoria that had slowly begun to fill him. The only word to escape her lips was 'Keeley'.

"Oh. My. God." Melissa looked at her mother with terror-filled eyes. Her mother's sight was definitely somewhere else, the eyes were dilated and unfocused. Cameron flew out of the room, ending up in the waiting room kneeling at his father's feet. He gazed at the little girl sitting on his dad's lap and breathed a sigh of relief. Whatever was going to happen, had not occurred yet.

Cameron would not leave Keeley's side until the danger had passed and he had changed her future. He would spend every moment learning how to control the physical realm. Cameron would not be able to save her if he was unable to make those around him feel his presence or move objects to prevent her from being taken.

Keeley was oblivious to his fear. She was nestled snuggly against her grandfather's chest, eyes closed and breathing gently. Cameron placed his hand over Keeley's, "I won't let anyone hurt you, Keeley. I will be your knight in shining armour."

Cameron looked at his father, taking in the stress lines that ran across his face. He wanted to put his dad's mind at ease but knew he couldn't do that while Keeley was in danger. His mother's visions had come closely together. Cameron hoped that meant the threat to Keeley would present itself soon and that he might just be able to reattach himself to his body before he found his name burned onto the reaper's list.

His dad's head rested on the wall behind him. His eyes were closed as his hand gently caressed Keeley's back as she slept in his arms. Cameron wondered if there was such a thing as Fate because if there was, he or she needed a swift kick up the backside. His parents didn't deserve this. Neither did his sister. To take David from them while he was still in his prime, and then allow Cameron to be involved in a serious accident was one thing, but for Keeley to be kidnapped by some creep was exceptionally cruel. If Wang Cho returned, Cameron would ask him. In the meantime, he needed to work on his skills so that he could protect Keeley when the time came.

Cameron walked down the hallway to the water dispenser. He brought up the memory of a scene in the movie 'Ghost' where Sam was trying to learn how to manipulate matter. He hoped the lessons Sam was given in the film would work for Cameron and that he would promptly pick up the skills required. After what seemed like hours, but was mere minutes, Cameron stopped trying and walked away. He hadn't given up on the idea. He was just taking a break to recharge his energy levels.

He wandered down the hallway, passing through the doors to an elevator. Cameron turned around and faced the front, moving into a sitting position on the floor. The confined space was comforting, the silence allowing him to think. Cameron had never felt so alone. He was surrounded by people, but other than Keeley wasn't able to communicate with any of them. He longed for the touch of another human being, to receive love and comfort that could only be secured through physical contact. The world had lost its colour, making it dull and leaving him feeling depressed.

A quick shake of the head cleared the harmful content that was crowding his thoughts. He didn't have time to wallow in self-pity. His mother had received a vision while he was present and turned him into a believer. There was no way she could have made that up. She hadn't even known he was in the room. Regardless of the issues that were keeping the women from leaning on one another for support, his mother would not have said the things she did in front of Melissa out of spite. She would not hurt her daughter in that way. So the vision must be real, and he needed to put Keeley's needs before his own. If that meant that he saved her, but wasn't able to protect himself, so be it.

The doors to the elevator opened, taking him by surprise. His jumpy reaction brought a smile to his lips. Raising his head, he was disappointed to see he was in the company of Wang Cho. "Have you come to take me away?" Cameron jumped to his feet, ready to flee.

"Not yet. I have come to remind you that the path you are on is heading in the wrong direction. There is the faintest outline of your name on my parchment." Wang turned the page around for Cameron's viewing. "You have made a decision that has set you on this course. If you don't change your mind, I will be back to reap your soul."

"I can't. There is more than my life at stake."

"Everything is not always as it seems. Your decision has a domino effect, Cameron. Your decision affects the lives of others tangled in your life's web."

"Which is exactly why I can't return just yet. Can't you buy me some time?"

"This is not like the movie 'Heart and Souls'. This is real life. I am overstepping my boundaries as it is. Whatever it is you think you have to do, is not worth risking your life for. You are not meant to be here, in the in-between. It is my opinion that you will not be able to function as you did before. I believe that you will begin to lose track of time once you no longer have anyone to hold your attention, and will forget the reason you have decided to remain a phantasm. The longer you stay a phantasm, the more chance your body will die which will bring on catastrophic consequences that I am not allowed to discuss with you. I cannot offer you any more assistance than I already have, Cameron. I hope you change your mind and reconnect with your body. I do not wish to have to see you again for many years to come."

Wang Cho faded away. Cameron blinked his eyes, wondering how that was possible. Had their conversation taken place, or had Cameron finally lost his grip on reality? Was the fact that he was in spirit form changing his perception of the world? Is that why the world had lost its colour? There were so many questions floating around in his head, he felt he would go mad if he weren't able to stop his mind from over-thinking things.

It was time to continue his attempts at manipulating the physical realm. Cameron left the elevator and returned to the water dispenser. He concentrated on separating the bottom cup from the others wedged in the cylindrical cup holder hanging off the side of the machine. "Come on, Cameron," he muttered. "All you've got to do is make the cup drop. Let gravity be your friend."

When that task seemed to take up too much energy, he decided to change tack. His focus turned to the tap that allowed the water to flow. He pictured the plastic lever rising, and when that didn't work, he imagined it being pulled down. With a frustrated sigh, he turned in a circle and began muttering words of positivity before trying again.

Feeling his energy fading, he wandered down the hallway and into his room. He glanced at his body with little curiosity before swinging his gaze to his sister. She held his hand tightly in her own. Her head rested against his arm, and her eyes were closed. A quick look at his mother had him jerking in surprise. She looked like she was having another vision.

What Cameron couldn't see was that the Reaper was giving Karen a 'vision' that Cameron's soul was outside his body and if it did not return shortly, he would die. If he dies, he will not be available to protect Keely. She realised that Cameron needed an incentive to return to his body. She was sitting on the chair, fiddling with Cameron's phone. "How did you get hold of that?" he stammered, looking at the device with longing. Could he manipulate the keys to type out a message? Perhaps that would be easier than trying to lift a cup into thin air.

His mother pushed a few buttons and placed the phone to her ear. Who was she ringing? His sister and father were here.

Twelve

Candice was feeling quite annoyed while she watched a movie with her parents. She could understand that Cameron might not want to text he was safe while in the company of his friends. Though, admittedly by now, he was at home with his family and could spare a few minutes to let her know he was okay. Especially after her witnessing the hostility that had existed between Adrian and himself.

She had no idea what was happening in the movie. Her thoughts were too focused on Cameron to follow the storyline. She couldn't even state with certainty the names of the main characters. Realising she was wasting her time, she decided to wait until an ad came on the screen before excusing herself. She wouldn't be able to concentrate until she had contacted him and confirmed he was okay. By then, she would probably be angry enough to give him a piece of her mind for scaring her unnecessarily.

She took her phone into the bedroom and brought contact details up on the screen. She stared at the numbers, contemplating the fact that she was worried about somebody she hardly knew. "You had better not hurt my feelings, Cameron . . ." She realised she didn't even know his last name. Something she would rectify when she spoke to him. She pressed the dial button and waited for him to answer. The phone rang out before it was answered. Before she could redial, her mother knocked on her door. Candice took one look at her mother's concerned face and braced herself for what was to come.

"May I come in, Candice?"

"Of course," she replied, stepping back to allow entry.

"Come sit with me," her mother suggested, gripping her by the elbow, and guiding her to a couple of chairs in the corner of the room. "This may not be of concern to you, Candice, and I am sorry if this will upset you unnecessarily."

"What is it, Mum?"

"A news report came on the television a few minutes ago about a serious accident this afternoon in Dennings Hill. I only mention it because it involved a black V8 sedan and teenagers who were travelling home from Wotomba."

"Oh my God," Candice said, jumping up from the chair to pace the floor. She flicked her hands continuously in an attempt to shake off the thoughts that were running through her head. "Did they say who was involved?" she asked as tears gathered in her eyes.

"No. I think they are still contacting their family members. Candice, I think you should prepare yourself . . ."

Her phone started ringing. She snatched it from her bed and looked at the screen. A grin spread across her face as she faced her mother. "It's Cameron," she said, accepting the call. "Hello Cameron," her voice reflected her relief. A frown crossed her face as she listened. She sank on to the edge of her bed and cried. Sarah walked over to her daughter and took the phone. She placed it against her ear and introduced herself, "This is Sarah, Candice's mother. To whom am I speaking?"

"Hello Sarah, my name is Karen. I am the mother of Cameron, a friend of your daughter."

"How is he? I just saw a report on the news. Was he involved in the accident they mentioned?"

"I'm afraid so. I won't speak ill of the dead, but I certainly wish Cameron had made some better choices today."

"Candice told me the driver was upset that she liked your son more than him."

"I'm not sure what the circumstances are surrounding the accident, and I am sorry I didn't contact you first. I didn't have a surname to try to track you down. The skating rink wouldn't hand out personal information about Candice to me, as they shouldn't. I'll leave it up to you, what you tell her. Two of the boys died on impact. The three in the back, including my Cameron, are in the Intensive Care Unit fighting for their lives. The doctors are confident they can pull Cameron through. They have placed him in an induced coma."

"And the others?"

"They can't discuss their prognosis with me. All I know is they are still hanging in there."

"I suppose Candice will want to see him. Would that be okay with you?"

"Of course. I would love to meet her and have her sit with Cameron. She might be just what he needs to pull through. The nurses, however, won't allow her in. Only immediate family members are allowed to visit. Would you have any objection to her wearing my mother's ring and pretending to be his fiancé?"

"I don't know about that, Karen."

"That's fine. I'm sure Candice won't mind waiting until he is out of the woods and transferred to a ward before visiting with him."

"That's not fair."

"What do you mean?"

"Using emotional blackmail like that."

"I am not trying to be cruel, Sarah. I am merely trying to get around hospital rules so the young ones can be together. Even if Cameron may not know she is there. We don't know if he can feel it when we touch him or hear our voices when we talk to him. I'd like to think he can, and it reminds him just how much we love him. Anything we can do to give him the desire to continue his fight to live."

"I don't think Candice's presence will make much difference to his prognosis. She barely knows him."

"Cameron has a huge crush on your daughter, Sarah. You would be surprised at the difference a visit from her would make."

"What are you talking about?" Candice tugged on her mother's arm. "I want to see him, Mum."

Sarah glanced at her daughter, raising a finger to her lips. Candice spun around and sat back on the edge of her bed. She was nineteen years old and more than capable of making her own decisions. The trouble was, she wasn't yet independent. She still lived at home and was forced to follow her parent's rules. She had a driver's licence but couldn't afford a car, and had to borrow her parent's vehicle to get around in. This was dependent on whether they approved of her destination.

Candice sighed. Surely her mother would allow her to go to the hospital to see him. If she didn't go, would Fate be so cruel as to snatch him away before she had a chance to really get to know him?

The sound of her mother's voice roused Melissa from her sleep. She lifted her head and wiped the drool from her mouth. With a confused frown, she uttered the word, "Mother?"

"Yes, it's me, honey. We are in the hospital, remember?"

Melissa looked down and saw Cameron lying prone on the bed. Unwanted images flickered through her mind causing her to gasp and place her head in her hands. Her mother walked around the side of the bed to lay her hand on Melissa's shoulder. "It'll be okay, Lissy. Candice is coming tomorrow. He won't have any other option than to wake up with the three of us hounding him to get better."

Melissa's muffled laughter was softer than that of her sniffling nose. A tissue appeared below her arm, which was gratefully taken. She gently wiped her nose, refusing to blow it and bring her dignity into further disrepute. Melissa lifted her head, "Thank you."

"You're welcome," her mother patted her shoulder before returning to her seat. "Cameron is going to survive this," she muttered as she shuffled her feet.

"How do you know?"

"They are going to get married, Cameron and Candice," she said, nodding her head in his direction. "I've seen it."

"Was that before or after you saw the accident?"

"It doesn't matter."

"Sure, it does. The accident could have changed the future you saw."

"I am confident that Candice will pull him out of his coma and they will have a long, happy life together."

"If that is true, then tell me this. Is Keeley going to suffer terribly at the hands of a monster?"

Her mother lowered her head. "I haven't seen that far ahead."

"What did you see?"

"Keeley strapped to a chair with zip ties. She has a blindfold over her eyes made from a black material, and she is screaming for Cameron to come and save her."

Melissa felt gutted. Not only was she sure that this would come to pass, her daughter believed more in her uncle's superpowers than her own. She knew it was stupid to be upset that Keeley had called

Cameron's name, and yet she was. "Do you have any idea when this is going to happen?"

"No. I can tell you she is wearing her yellow pyjamas with the penguins."

"I'm afraid that doesn't help much. She loves them so much. I had to buy three pairs. She wears them to bed every night."

"At least we know she will be taken at night. What is she wearing now?"

"Her pyjamas," Melissa cried, banging Cameron's bed in her haste to get up. She raced for the door and threw it open without thought for anything else. The nurse in the room growled at her, but she didn't take heed. Melissa exited the room, calling her daughter's name. Her dad woke with a start, nearly tossing Keeley off his lap. "What's wrong?" he asked, gripping her tighter. Keeley whined with pain and fear. "Sorry, Pumpkin," he soothed. Looking back at Melissa, he continued, "Has something changed with Cameron's status?"

"No, Dad. I'm sorry to startle you. I was worried about the pair of you sitting out here on uncomfortable chairs. Why don't you go and sit with Cameron for a while? I'll take Keeley home, so she gets some proper sleep in a bed."

"Are you sure, Love? I can take her home with me and put her to bed. You can stay and keep your mother company."

"I appreciate the thought, but you need to spend some time with him, too. He is your son."

"I know," he said.

"Dad, he will make it or he won't. Your refusal to go in there is not going to change the outcome for him. It will affect the way you see yourself for the rest of your life. Do you want to try to wrap your heart in cotton wool to prevent the heartbreak that will come if he dies? Trust me, there is no possible way to prepare for something like that. Being forewarned of impending doom won't change the pain that is to come. If Cameron was to die, do you want to have to live with the fact that you abandoned him in his time of need, when you could have spent more time with him? You know that is where your mind will take you."

Her dad conceded she was right in her thinking. He allowed Melissa to take Keeley off his hands and rose with stiff legs. She gave him a kiss on the cheek, and he returned a kiss to her forehead. "See you in the morning," she said.

"Okay. Drive carefully."

"I will."

Keeley spotted Cameron standing behind Melissa. She placed her head on Melissa's shoulder and closed her eyes with a smile. Cameron was torn between staying with his dad and following Keeley home. There was something important he had to remember. He shuffled from foot to foot, his fingers moving through the air as though tapping a set of keys. "What is it?" he mumbled over and over. He watched his dad trundle towards his room then turned his head to watch Melissa walk towards the elevator. His eyes fell on Keeley, and he remembered. He had to stay with his niece to make sure she remained safe.

He glided above the floor, the elevators not registering his presence as he neared the closing doors. With a burst of speed, he passed through the doors and entered the cubicle that had begun its descent. A shiver wracked Melissa's body as the temperature dropped with his arrival. Cameron noticed the movement and realised his presence made those around him cold. He kept as much distance as he could between the girls and himself. That would be harder once they got to the car, he surmised.

An image of the boot popped into his consciousness. If he tucked himself into the boot for the ride home, his family should be insulated from the cold. Without the stimulation of people around him, Cameron lost track of time and the reason for his existence in that state. He bounced between the physical and ghostly planes until his name appeared more firmly on the reaper's list. At that time, the reaper decided to seek help to set the course of destiny back on the right path.

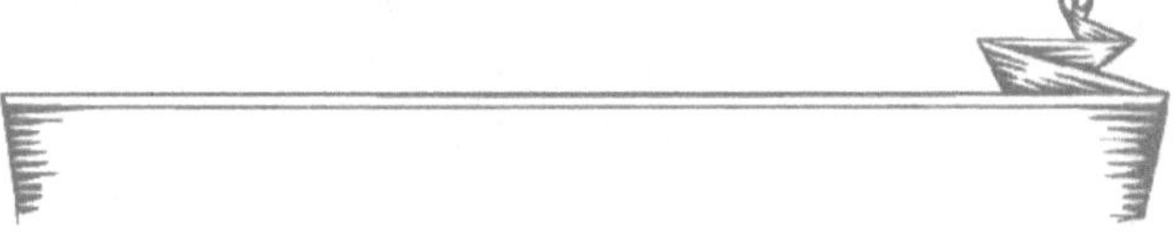

Thirteen

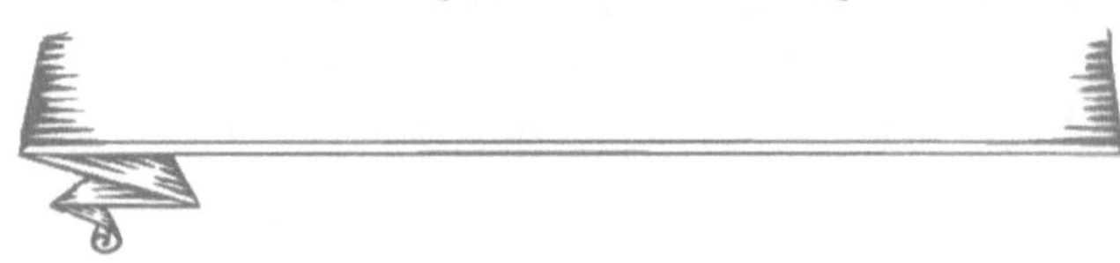

The courage of the young man before him could not be denied. Neither could the stupidity he was displaying in his course of action. It was swiftly becoming apparent that the boy was willing to risk his physical life over something that may not occur for months. A quick glance at his list showed that Cameron was quickly running out of time. Though it was forbidden to meddle with the wishes of Fate, the reaper could sense other forces were at play and was willing to put his neck on the line for the life of a boy whose end was coming prematurely.

With a wave of his hand, the three-piece-suit was replaced by the more traditional black hooded robe which was used as a source of intimidation when dealing with supernatural beings. To most, the robe served as a reminder that the reapers were as old as time and contained an infinite amount of power. They were the army of Destiny herself.

He ran his hands over the material, luxuriating in its silky softness. While the suit was more readily accepted by the humans when he first approached them, providing him with a chance to converse with the newly departed in a calm, reassuring manner, the material was stiff and scratchy against his weathered skin. With a raised hand, his scythe answered the command, sailing through the air to snuggle gently into the pocket provided by his curled fingers. A tap to the floor had him moving toward the location of the nearest Locator Fairy.

He travelled unseen across the Earth until he reached his destination. He waited patiently for the fairy to become aware of his presence, so he didn't frighten her unnecessarily. When the prickle of awareness moved over her skin, she lifted her head and gasped in fright anyway. It was a rare occurrence that a fairy had dealings with a reaper.

Wang raised his hand in a non-threatening manner. "Calm yourself, fairy. I mean you no harm. I come asking for your assistance in a delicate matter."

Tianna rose to her feet, letting go of the cherry blossom she'd held in her hand. Her wings carried her to a branch that would bring her near eye level with the reaper. All she could see was his face nestled inside the hood of the cloak. He was Asian in appearance with piercing brown eyes that stared at her as she assessed him. His mouth was turned up at the edges in amusement as she brazenly stood her ground, flicking her eyes over his features. "Aren't you a tall one," she muttered under her breath, calculating him to be nearing two and a half metres in height. "State your business, Reaper," she said bravely without a quiver in her voice.

He admired the muted tones of her long, lilac hair which hung in soft waves to her waist. His smile lengthened when her almond-shaped eyes with their violet centres flashed at him in defiance. She lifted her chin and placed her hands on her hips. She spread her legs slightly for better balance. Her outfit reminded him of those worn by the Valkyrie. Lots of bare skin to distract their enemy amid battle. Wang had to admit, the strategy was extremely effective.

"So much spirit in such a tiny being," he grinned, pointing a bony finger towards her. "My name is Wang Cho. I am pleased to make your acquaintance." He waited patiently for her to shake his digit, a scowl crossing his face as she simply stared at the appendage. "Beautiful, but sadly lacking in manners."

"I do not know you. Therefore, it is impossible to gauge whether your intentions are honourable or not. I am not going to make it easier for you to grab me by sticking out my arm."

"My lady, had I wanted to capture you, you would be tightly ensconced in my hand at this very moment."

Tianna tipped her head up as she considered his words. She had to admit that what he said was true. She had been warned over many centuries that their magic was not effective against death himself. "Then may I offer you my sincerest apologies," she held out her hand, hoping he was still willing to shake fingers with her. Wang Cho portrayed a solemn look as he accepted her apology.

"There, that wasn't so hard."

A scowl crossed her face as her hand returned to her hip. "I am a busy fairy, Reaper. What is it that you want from me?"

"I need the help of a Gatherer," he stated.

"Then go and find yourself one."

"I would if they could see me. Alas, they cannot."

"What do you mean? I can see you."

"You are a magical being. Of course, you can see me. Although the Gatherer's physiology has advanced far beyond that which was intended, they are still human at the core. Therefore cannot see a reaper until they are near the end of this journey and ready to begin their next."

"Has that ever happened?"

"Not yet," Wang admitted, thinking about the name that had recently appeared on his list. He hadn't come face to face with the Gatherer whose soul was soon to be reaped.

"What do you need me to do?"

"I need you to convince a Gatherer to help a young man whose soul was separated from his body during an accident."

"What are they supposed to do?"

"Convince him to return to his body before it is too late."

"What difference does it make? People die all the time."

"Yes, but it is not his time. A death out of sequence will rip the fabric of time and space to shreds. Chaos will reign, and portals that are meant to remain closed will tear open, releasing a horde of evil upon many worlds."

Tianna would have scoffed at his words if she hadn't seen the truth of it in his eyes. Gathering her thoughts, she paced along the length of the branch. "What is the boy?"

"He is a phantasm. Spiritual energy that is still attached to this realm."

"What is the difference between a phantasm, ghost, and poltergeist?"

"A phantasm is born out of an incident so traumatic that the spirit leaves the living body as a coping mechanism. It is usually only separated for a short time before it is drawn back to the body to enable healing. A ghost is a spirit which has refused to enter the next realm upon the body's death. This can be for numerous reasons; fear of the unknown, unfinished business, unwilling to leave loved ones, etcetera, etcetera. A poltergeist is born from a person who has suffered a violent death or has been among the living for too long. Revenge for their murder tarnishes the soul and turns it evil as does existing around the living and not being able to interact with them. My young man, Cameron, was involved in a terrible accident. He was not supposed to be in the vehicle at the time, which is why I need your help."

"I thought you weren't supposed to interfere with them."

"I am not, but the fact that Cameron was where he was not meant to be, indicates something else is at work here. I cannot stand by and watch the end of everything come to pass because I was not willing to step in and fix what wasn't meant to be. I sent a vision to his mother of a future without him in it as soon as I became aware that destiny had been changed. Unfortunately, that wasn't enough.

"She is either unwilling to believe the magnitude of the events that will occur should he refuse to meld with his body, or he is unwilling to listen to her warning. Whatever the issue seems to be, Cameron continues to refuse to merge with his physical self, meaning his body will eventually die. It cannot survive without the soul, even with the advances of medicine the humans have achieved."

"You still haven't told me how a Gatherer can help. What are they supposed to do?"

"Convince Cameron to return to the living. The Gatherers are protectors of humans. They have powers that only select humans will ever manage to acquire. Their abilities will allow them to see him, communicate with him. They will be able to show him that they are more than capable of doing whatever it is Cameron feels he has to do before he can return to his body. A Gatherer is our only hope of saving the living from Hell itself."

"Where will they find him?"

"His is currently in Dennings Hill. His spirit spends most of his time hovering around his sister and her young daughter."

"Which one do you think he is attached to?"

"I believe it is the young girl. She can see him."

"Then get her to help him."

"I can't. She is three years old. Besides, I think she is the reason he is refusing to return to his body."

"That gives us something to work with."

"I'm sorry, my lady. Once you have connected your Gatherer with Cameron, you must have no further contact with them. There are other things at play that you must not interfere with."

"I am a Locator Fairy. I locate creatures that are not of this world. Locating Cameron is going to be more difficult than you think, considering he is of human spirit, and of this world. If the Gatherer loses him, I will need to be close by to help them re-locate the boy."

"You must not impede the Gatherers actions. They will have no trouble locating his presence once initial contact is made."

"And you know this how?"

"I am a reaper. I see all."

"Then you know who put Cameron in harm's way?"

"That I cannot see." He raised his finger to silence the comment he knew was coming. "Make haste to contact your Gatherer. Time is wasting."

"Are you telling me that I am wasting your time?"

He ignored her comment. "Cameron believes he has a mission to complete before he reconnects to the physical world. He is not dangerous, yet. That could change if he feels he is being forced to relinquish his quest. It is going to be extremely hard to persuade him to join his soul to his body. If your Gatherer fails to convince him, he *will die.*"

Tianna stood for a few seconds staring at the empty spot before her. She rubbed the skin on her arms, warming the bumps that had risen with his swift departure. She hoped that when she abandoned her Gatherer in the middle of a case, she'd be forgiven. They had a tenuous relationship which Tianna would like to improve.

She returned to her dwelling at the base of the tree to collect her spear and helmet, two items she never travelled without. She drank some nectar from a nasturtium flower, enjoying its peppery taste before leaving the park she lived in to locate the nearest available Gatherer. Tianna flew to the nearest electricity pole and landed on the tip.

She sent out a pulse of energy, then scanned the area for a response. The ripple faded into the darkness, moments before the sky erupted into waves of energy as other fairies picked up her pleas for assistance then forwarded the request with a pulse of their own. An answering signal was returned within minutes. A flare of light in pastel pink with swirling sparkles of silver lit up the sky to the south.

Tianna smiled. She had known Rochelle was the closest Gatherer to her position when talking to the reaper. What she hadn't known was whether Rochelle was available to take care of the phantasm. She waited patiently for the message to take shape. The beam fanned out into three streams, then curled into three spheres. One by one they exploded into tiny stars, shimmering for a few seconds before burning out. Tianna nodded her head, satisfied with the reply. Rochelle would arrive within three hours.

Tianna flew back to her tree and lay on her bed which was spun from the silk of a spider and resembled a hammock. She hadn't had much rest for a few days and decided to get in some shut-eye while she had the chance. A couple of hours later, she woke to gather her things. Inside her satchel, she placed a ripened strawberry which would travel better than her nasturtium flowers and provide fluids to keep her hydrated. She plucked two of the youngest mushrooms in the circle as they gave her a sustained burst of energy rather than the quick peak and trough that came with the more mature fungi.

Next, in the front pocket of the bag, she placed the homing device that Rochelle had given her after discovering Tianna had difficulty finding her way home from unknown localities. She snuffed out the lantern then stepped outside, locking the door that covered the hole in the trunk of her tree home.

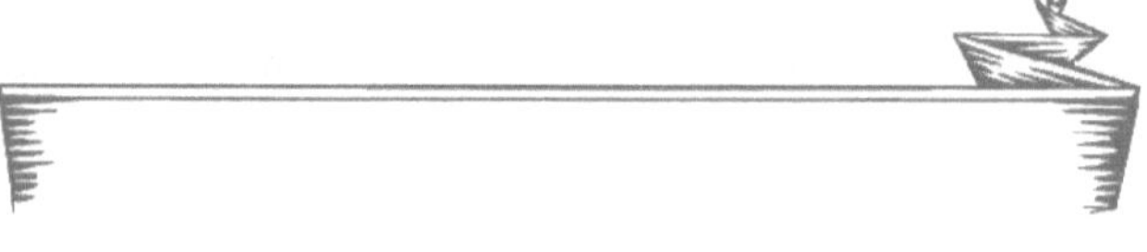

Rochelle gazed up at Toren as he gently stroked the side of her face. She lay nestled between his legs on a picnic blanket with her head resting lightly in his lap. "Open up ladybird," he grinned, waving a green, seedless grape across her mouth.

"If you don't stop feeding me while I am lying down, you are going to make me choke," she warned.

"Then I will have to give you mouth-to-mouth until you can breathe on your own. That might take a while, so you should think about eating carefully," he smirked.

"Are you trying to take advantage of the situation?" she gasped, attempting to lift herself into a sitting position.

"Now, now. Don't get your knickers in a knot," he scolded, placing both hands on her shoulders and nudging her back into position. "I wouldn't dream of placing your life at risk." He leaned forward and gave her an upside-down-kiss on her lips. "Hmmm, delicious."

"Me or the grapes?" she uttered playfully.

"Is there any competition?" he replied, aghast at her comment. Rochelle let out a deep sigh. "What was that for?"

"Have you ever felt that life was so perfect you must have died and gone to Heaven?" she queried.

"Every time I look at you," he answered truthfully.

"You are so corny," she said, raising her hand and slapping his arm.

"No, I mean it," he assured her. "Every time I catch a glimpse of you, my heart skips a beat with excitement."

"Really?"

"Really, truly." He delivered another kiss to her lips. This one lasting a few seconds longer than the previous. Rochelle rolled over, breaking off their kiss. She was conscious they were sitting in the middle of a park, surrounded by dozens of children on various play equipment. "Sometimes, I marvel at your restraint," he pouted.

"Are you trying to convince me that after nearly five hundred years of us dating, and three thousand years as a Gatherer, you have no self-control where intimacy is concerned? Liar," she laughed, crawling up onto her knees before seating herself in a cross-legged position facing him.

"We've been together for nearly five centuries?"

She stared at him with livid eyes, before the realisation that he was joking crossed her face. "Toren, you are such a . . ."

"Not in front of the children, love," he reminded her, leaning forward and placing a finger over her lips. "I have been counting the days with amazement that you have stayed with me for so long. I can't believe you haven't become bored with me."

"Toren, I will love you until the end of my days and then longer."

"What about the nights?" he waggled his eyebrows.

Rochelle burst into laughter. "Yeah, them too. Why don't we get out of here?"

"And go where?" His pupils dilated as he gripped her beneath the chin and pulled her towards him.

"The beach. I have the strangest desire to look for mermaids." She could hear his heartbeat pick up speed. Looking for mermaids was their code phrase for skinny-dipping.

"Hmmm that sounds like fun," he murmured against her lips. "I've heard there are thousands of people flocking to the ocean today to escape the heat. Why don't we head inland? There's a lovely secluded spot along the Darling River I'd love to share with you," he stated.

"You've never taken me there before," Rochelle squinted suspiciously.

"Well I'm taking you there now, *if* you want to go," his voice sounded a bit gruff.

"Are there mermaids there?"

"You bet."

"Sounds lovely," Rochelle said, rising to her feet. She started packing the picnic items away when a young voice reached their ears.

"Mummy, can we go and see the mermaids too?" a girl with large brown eyes and short dark hair implored her mother.

"Don't be silly, Patricia. There are no such things as mermaids."

"But those people . . ."

"Come along, Patricia. Some people say the silliest things," her mother informed her.

Rochelle and Toren glanced at one another, passing a private thought through mind-link before returning to the task of packing their stuff up and loading it into the car. Mermaids were real. They had captured a number of them over the years and sent them to the planet, Mystique, for safekeeping.

Rochelle placed her foot on the step of the Landcruiser before hauling herself into the passenger seat. Toren figured she needed his assistance and set his hand on her bottom, giving a gentle push. Her lips twitched as a smile tried to break free. Rochelle raised her left hand and covered the lower part of her face from view. Toren climbed into the driver's seat and glanced in her direction. "Something wrong?" His eyes sparkled with mischief.

"Not at all," she replied, glancing out the window. Rochelle caught a glimpse of the energy ripple that was swiftly approaching before it crashed into her body and washed over her skin. The door rocked on its hinges as she launched herself out of the vehicle. Toren was by her side in seconds. They deciphered the message contained within the pulse, their muscles relaxing as the information was released. The creature that needed to be dealt with was a level five, mischievous but not dangerous.

Toren hoped that Rochelle would be willing to take on the case. He was in the middle of adding the finishing touches to a cottage he had built to celebrate their five-hundredth-year together as a couple.

"I've got this," she stated with her hands on her hips, bracing for an argument.

"Okay," he replied, being careful not to answer too quickly, or show how relieved he was currently feeling.

Rochelle's eyes narrowed at his response. They were highly competitive, neither prepared to give in so easily when a case cropped up. "That was easy," she stated slowly, peering at him intently.

"It's a level five," he answered in a complacent tone. "Hardly worth fighting over, don't you think?"

"If you say so," she said, moving a few metres away to send her response.

"How do you think I should travel, Toren? There is a lot of traffic congestion on the road at this time of the day. I love running freely as a German Shepherd but it is a long way. It would probably be less stressful to morph into a bird of prey, and travel by air. What do you think?"

"Wait, Rochelle. There's something I want to give you before you go." She raised her eyebrows while waiting for him to retrieve the object. "It's not here," he stated. "Get in the car, it won't take long."

Rochelle gazed in the direction the pulse had come from. "Tianna is waiting. I told her I would be there in three hours." "It won't take long, Rochelle," he repeated with the puppy-dog-eye look. A strategy that always had him getting his own way.

"Fine," she sighed, wishing she could resist that look.

Once again, she was helped into the car, though she didn't need assistance. The move lightening the pressure she felt to respond immediately to another's request for her presence. She buckled up her seatbelt and wondered what gift could be so extraordinary that it couldn't wait until she returned.

Rochelle frowned when they pulled into his driveway and stopped. "Aren't you going to put it away?"

"No," he turned the key and undid his seatbelt.

"Are you going out again?"

"I'm not going to sit at home and twiddle my thumbs until you return from your assignment, Rochelle."

"I didn't think you would," she retorted, her frown deepening as he led her towards the garage door. "If we are going in this way, why wouldn't you just put your car away?"

"Maybe there is something in the way," his exasperated voice indicated the darkening of his mood. His feelings of excitement were dulling, and disappointment was filling the void. This wasn't how he'd pictured the scene in his mind.

The roll-a-door slid up at the touch of a remote control held in his hand, slowly revealing a vibrant blue vehicle hidden inside. Rochelle could feel the tension of excitement building in her body. Her eyes were riveted to the object being exposed. Her breath caught in her throat and she started to panic that this was the gift Toren was planning to give to her. A Ferrari didn't come cheap, and she felt she had done nothing to deserve such a magnificent machine. All she had managed to achieve was to love a man that she couldn't bear to live without.

The more she thought about this, the more she began to panic that the car wasn't her new toy. After getting her hopes up that he was giving her the car, how would she respond if he were to gift her with something like a locket containing their photos, or a pen with her name engraved on it? A gift that was wonderful and would be treasured by her, but not on the same level that a Ferrari would be.

She had to pull herself together. Toren was the most significant gift she could ever hope to receive, and he was all hers. If she were able to spend the rest of her life with him, then everything else would pale in comparison. The feeling of panic melted away. A calmness blanketed her, allowing her to return to normal. She turned her attention to Toren, to find his focus centred on her. She blushed, her face becoming more attractive with the rosy hue staining her cheeks. Her smouldering grey eyes gazed at him questioningly. Her lips slightly parted with anticipation.

"She's yours," he said quietly, the intensity of his love depicted in the way he looked at her, his posture and his tone.

"Are you sure you want to give her to me, and not keep her for yourself?"

"You are worth more to me than life itself. I have noticed your obsession with this particular vehicle and the lengths you have gone to, keeping it a secret."

"Such as?"

"If I told you, I wouldn't be able to deduce the next thing that grabs your attention and refuses to let go."

"You are the only thing that truly has my attention. You are the first thing I think of when I wake up, and the last thing I think of before going to sleep."

"You are equating me to an object?" he asked crestfallen.

"That's not what I meant. It's just a saying, 'cause if I said person, it wouldn't make sense when we are discussing things."

Toren burst into laughter. "My goodness you get yourself into a verbal mess," he chuckled at the words.

Rochelle pursed her lips and stormed towards the car. Toren grabbed her around the waist and pulled her against him. She felt the firmness of his body and melted into his embrace. He pulled her hair to the side with his other hand and kissed her on the back of her neck. "I love you, Rochelle. For now and always."

"I love you, too," she moaned.

He let her go. "I've had a few modifications done to the vehicle. The car is controlled by your voice commands. You are the only one who can start it. If anyone else attempts to steal the car, they will be blasted with a few hundred volts of electricity. It won't kill them, but it will hurt like hell."

"Anything else I should know?" Rochelle slid into the driver's seat, the smile reaching her eyes.

"Yes, we will christen her when you get home. You have a job to get to," his laughter stopped. "Be careful. There are risks associated with level five creatures that we aren't always aware of."

"I know, Toren. I've been doing this for three millennia."

"Come back to me soon."

"I'll be back before our anniversary," she assured him.

With a farewell kiss, she started the car and began her journey. Thanks to the beautiful weather, she chose to leave the top down.

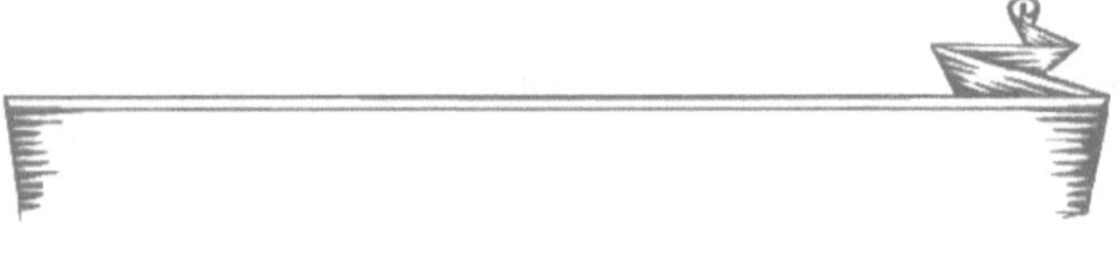

Fifteen

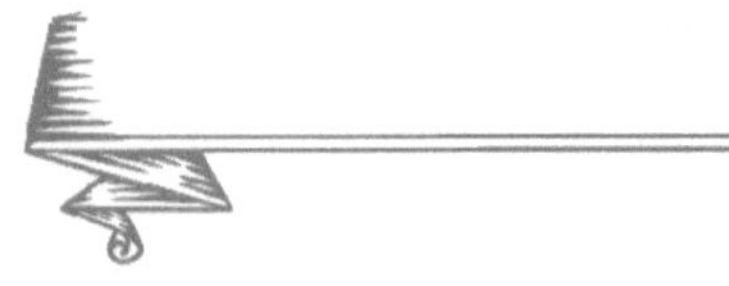

Tianna's timing was impeccable. By the time she completed her tasks and locked the front door, she spotted Rochelle walking towards her. Rochelle was a force to be reckoned with.

She had the face of an angel. A woman that you instinctively trusted from the moment you laid eyes on her. But, there was a dangerous side to the woman approaching. A hint of which could be seen if you looked deep enough into her eyes. Her hair was styled into twin braids.

She wore the official outfit that all Gatherers were given when they chose this lifestyle. It was made of a material that could change to suit the needs of the wearer. For the meeting between Gatherer and Locator Fairy, the suit appeared as a form-fitting tank-top with mid-shin-length running pants and a pair of white socks and pink sneakers on her feet. To anyone glancing over, Rochelle would seem to be a jogger, out for a run in the park.

Tianna fluttered in front of Rochelle's face, close enough to be heard, with an enormous grin on her face. "Hello, Early Bird. It is so lovely to see you again."

"Hey, Tianna. You look ready for business."

Rochelle was not surprised to see Tianna's helmet perched firmly on her head nor the spear nestled snugly in her hand. She was dressed in a deep green pantsuit.

"How's Toren?"

"Healthy and awesome as always."

Tianna took note of the way Rochelle's grey eyes sparkled with affection upon the mention of her boyfriend's name and wished she had someone to cause that reaction in herself. "What creature is currently terrorising your neck of the woods, Tianna? I'm here and ready for action."

"Well, actually Rochelle, it's not a creature at all. I had a visit from a reaper who wants you to help a young phantasm reattach itself to its body."

Rochelle turned around and began walking away. Tianna flew after her. "Where are you going?"

"Sorry, Tianna. I am not getting involved in reaper business."

"You won't be breaking any rules. In fact, you will be helping to reset the balance. According to the reaper, Cameron wasn't even supposed to be in the car in which he had his accident."

"That doesn't make sense."

"Let me tell you everything he said. If you still want to walk away, I won't stop you. There are other Gatherers I can call on for help."

Rochelle held out her palm to provide comfort for Tianna while she related the conversation she'd had with the reaper.

"What does he think he can accomplish as a phantasm that he can't as a human?"

"I'm not sure."

"It takes months, if not years for the departed to let go of their humanity enough to learn the art of manipulating energy without their physical form. Cameron will be well and truly dead by then."

"Then I guess you have your starting point in persuading him to join the land of the living. If you are going to hang around, that is."

"Yes, I am going to hang around. I don't have to talk with the reaper, do I?"

"Considering the fact you can't see him, I'd say that's a no," Tianna rolled her eyes and fluttered her wings.

A scowl spread across Rochelle's face. "Don't you roll your eyes at me!"

"I'll do what I damned well please," Tianna replied.

"Okay. Keep your shirt on," laughed Rochelle. "Where do you want to start?"

"The reaper said the boy was in the hospital at Dennings Hill."

Rochelle pulled a mobile phone from a side pocket in her pants and brought up the street maps on the screen. She typed 'Dennings Hill Hospital' into the search and discovered there were two in that town. "Dennings Hill has a public and a private hospital. Let me do another search to see if I can determine which one took in accident victims around the time Cameron was hurt." Tianna waited patiently while Rochelle completed her search. "Hmmm, they both received patients around that time," Rochelle grumbled with frustration.

"Let's start at the public hospital. If he was sent there and then transferred to the private hospital, there will be a paper trail. If he is still there, your work can begin."

"It shouldn't be too hard to discern which patient is lying around spiritless."

"So what do you need me for?" Tianna asked.

"I will be able to see what he looks like, but won't be able to tap into his energy until contact is made with his consciousness. That is where you come in. I'll need you to locate his soul."

"As I told the reaper, we locate non-indigenous creatures that are harmful to the human race. Cameron is human. How am I supposed to locate him?"

"I am hoping his unusual circumstance will ping your radar, Tianna."

"Wouldn't that have happened already?"

"Not necessarily. At this stage, he is a danger to himself, not others. It is only when his body dies that all Hell will break loose. What do you think makes this guy's life so important? Why would some unknown entity have taken such an interest in one person?"

"According to Wang, the fabric of time itself will rip apart if Cameron dies when it is not his time. Perhaps it didn't matter who the victim was. Only that there was one."

"It has to be connected to Cameron somehow. There has to be a reason that events were manipulated in such a way that he was present in that car when the collision occurred."

"The reaper reckons a wave of evil will be unleashed across many worlds. Maybe the boy has a connection to the occult."

Rochelle raised her eyebrows, "We contain evil entities all the time. What makes this boy any different?"

"I don't know, but while the reaper was talking to me, I pictured The Cleanse we were involved in but multiplied it by one hundred. Maybe we should concentrate on returning Cameron to his body and then work out who separated him in the first place?"

Rochelle looked shocked. Three millennia ago, selected humans were exposed to radiation which forced their bodies to take a leap in evolution. As a result, the Battle Stars were born. They were used to round up an assortment of monsters that were preying on the human species and relocate them to another planet. It had been dangerous, gruelling work, something she didn't want to have to repeat. The gravity of the situation quickly pressed down on Rochelle's shoulders.

"You are right. We had better hurry to get this phantasm back where he belongs."

Tianna flew beside Rochelle as they made their way to her car. Tianna was expecting Rochelle to transform into a dog, her usual method of getting around when on a case. Her eyes almost bugged out of her head when Rochelle stopped in front of the Ferrari.

"Is this yours?" Tianna squealed with delight.

"It sure is. A gift from Toranthian."

"Wow! Are you serious?" Tianna asked wide-eyed.

Rochelle laughed, "He can afford it."

Tianna landed on the passenger seat, wriggling around until she was comfortably seated. She took a deep breath, closing her eyes with delight as the smell of new leather tickled her senses. Tianna's hands caressed the material beneath them. While Rochelle asked the car to start, Tianna tried her best to contain her excitement. She was afraid she would explode with happiness. Rochelle peeled her little beauty away from the curb and roared up to the corner. Tianna sat on the seat with her arms above her head and her fists punching the air. Her scream of pleasure became lost to the sound of the engine.

Rochelle parked the car and stepped out of the vehicle. She undid the braids and ran her fingers through her hair. She bunched her hair up into a ponytail and then twirled it around her fingers, forming a bun. She grabbed one of the ties from her wrist and secured her hair in place. Her outfit transformed into a nurses uniform and her shoes became comfortable black leather flats. She walked to the elevator and waited for the doors to open. "Are you ready?" she asked Tianna.

Tianna nodded and flew behind Rochelle, nestling her legs into the strands of Rochelle's hair. She tucked her arms in front of her body and kept her head straight. She flattened her wings, so the pattern was visible to all. Anybody taking a cursory glance at the back of Rochelle's head would see a decorative bow situated above the bun. Only a closer inspection would reveal something very peculiar about the fashion accessory.

"Can you breathe?" Rochelle queried.

"Yes, but please don't dilly-dally. I like to see where I am going," Tianna advised through mind-link.

"Got it."

Rochelle rode the elevator to the seventh floor and exited with all the confidence of a nurse who had every right to be there. She walked to the nurse's station and sorted through the charts. She was surprised to see it unattended but wasn't going to look a gift horse in the mouth. There must have been some kind of emergency that required the assistance of all available staff. Hopefully, it wasn't her boy.

There were only two young people in Intensive Care, neither of them named Cameron. "We've got the wrong hospital, Tianna." Rochelle left. Nobody had batted an eyelid. The private hospital was a ten-minute drive. Her outfit changed colour to match the nurses that were exiting. "Change of shift. That could work to our advantage." The private sector was more consistent with its staffing and more likely to notice an unfamiliar face.

Intensive Care was on the fourth floor, and there were three nurses situated at the nurses' desk. Rochelle glanced around, looking for another way in. There wasn't any that she could see. She would have to get past the nurses at the desk before she could begin her search for Cameron. She didn't want to mess with their minds, although there would be no choice for the one who remained in his room.

Rochelle sought out the frequency of the electrical current that ran through the wiring on the floor. She traced the pathways until she found a wire leading to a heart monitor. With a small tweak to the power supply, she was able to trip the alarm built into the machine. The nurses dropped what they were doing and ran for the room.

Rochelle wasted no time in hunting down Cameron's room. She followed the path that led to the boy without an energy signature. A man with a small child slept on a chair along the wall outside the room. When she opened the door, she saw a woman, who she assumed was his mother, with her head on the bed and eyes closed. Rochelle entered quietly and gently laid her hand on his forehead. Several scenes flashed through her mind, filled with powerful emotions. She quickly withdrew her hand and inhaled sharply.

The emotional pain that lay inside the young man was overwhelming. As she left the room, she raised her fist to her mouth to contain the sob that threatened to escape. With tears spilling from her eyes, she found herself gazing into those of the young girl. Keeley lifted her head from her grandfather's chest and said, "Why you cwying?"

"I just felt sad," Rochelle replied, glancing at the man.

"You here to see Uncle Camwon?"

"Yes, I'm here to help him."

"He don't need help. He's happy."

"How do you know that?"

"He is smiling beside you, but he likes being inbisible."

"Here's here, now?" Rochelle looked around.

"He inbisible to me too, now," she shrugged her shoulders.

"Do you think your mum and dad would like to see him?"

"My mum would. My dad is dead."

"Who are you talking to, Pumpkin?"

"The lady," she returned her gaze to her grandfather and placed her fingers against his eyes to pry open his eyelids.

Grandfather chuckled, raising his hands to grab hold of her arms. "Stop now, so I can open them myself," he said.

Keeley giggled as she peered into his face. "See the lady?"

He turned his head. "Yes, I see the lady," he smiled and held out his hand. "My name is Johnathon. This is Keeley, my granddaughter. Her mother is at university, and my wife, Karen, is inside with Cameron," his head dipped sideways to indicate the room ahead.

"My name is Rochelle. I am a physiotherapist. I've come to do some body manipulation to prevent muscle atrophy and bed sores. Can you confirm how long he has been here, please?"

"Three days."

"I won't stay any longer than is necessary, but your wife will have to leave the room."

"That's fine. She needs to get up and move her legs anyway. She's been sitting in there for many hours."

"Why don't you go grab yourselves a cup of coffee at the refectory? I'll come get you when I'm done."

"Thanks, Miss."

"Rochelle."

"Rochelle," he nodded.

"We'll be seeing more of each other, I am sure." She re-entered the room, and a few minutes later, Karen walked out. She was calm and ready to spend some time with her husband, thanks to the suggestion placed in her mind by Rochelle. The nurse on duty went about her duties as though Rochelle wasn't there. Tianna removed herself from Rochelle's hair and fluttered to Cameron's chest.

She walked up the bed sheet until she reached his chin where she turned around and sat cross-legged, her wings nestled tightly against his skin. She closed her eyes and placed her arms along her thighs, hands facing up. She sent out her psyche, looking for a lost soul.

"Got anything?" Rochelle asked.

"Sure. There are a lot of unattached souls floating through the corridors."

Rochelle looked at the ceiling and counted to ten. "Have you found *our* soul?"

"Not yet, and don't roll your eyes at me," Tianna replied.

"I didn't roll my eyes," Rochelle said indignantly.

She picked up Cameron's hand and rubbed her fingers over his knuckles. "So young," she murmured. She dived into his mind and searched for the last memories contained within his brain. She saw the events leading up to the crash and then darkness. There was no more once the soul had become detached from the body. She got a taste of his emotions; love for family, interest in Candice, trepidation of Adrian's intentions, hope for the future, sadness over the past. A complex set for somebody who had barely lived. One thing that stood out from the rest was his devotion to his niece.

"*I've found him*," Tianna squealed, rising to her feet.

"Where?"

"*He is standing in the middle of an intersection downtown.*"

"What would he be doing there?"

"*People who die are quite often drawn to the place where they died.*"

"But he didn't die," Rochelle said.

"*No, but he did get separated from his body. Do you want to meet with him?*"

"That's what we're here for." Rochelle tucked his hand under the blankets. She waited for Tianna to settle herself in her hair before opening the door. She made her way to the refectory to let Cameron's parents know she was done. Then she drove to his location to try to convince him to return to the living.

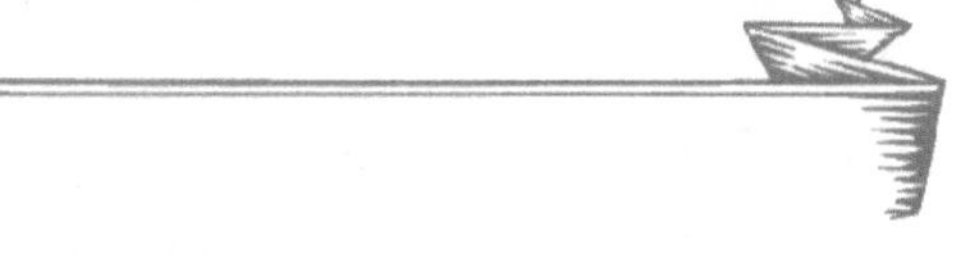

Sixteen

Rochelle parked the car a few houses from the corner and walked to the edge of the channelling. She surveyed the area without success. Cameron was nowhere to be seen. She looked up and down both streets to no avail. "Is he gone?" she asked Tianna.

"No, he is still here," she confirmed.

"Where? I don't see anything."

"Is it safe to come out?"

"Yes, I can't see anybody."

Tianna fluttered in front of Rochelle and pointed a little to the right. "He's there, standing on the bitumen."

"I don't see him. I thought the reaper said I would be able to see him."

"He did. I was supposed to lead you to his soul and then leave you to it. How am I supposed to do that if you can't see him?"

"Can you get in touch with the reaper?"

"I don't know. I can try."

"You do that while I give Starlight a call."

Tianna fluttered over to the leaves of the nearest tree seeking cover. She sent out an energy pulse, hoping she had directed it to reapers only. The last thing she wanted was for the other fairies to pick up the distress call. Rochelle pulled her superiors up on speed dial, hoping to get some answers. With a stroke of luck, Sophia was the one who answered the phone.

"Hey, Rochelle. What can I do for you?"

"Do you know anything about phantasms?"

"Can't say that I do. Would you like me to ask around?"

"Not particularly. I'd like to keep this on the down-low if possible."

"Why is that? Won't you require assistance for the removal of the beast?"

"Not this time. I will need you to be prepared for a mass invasion if I fail the mission."

"Whoa there, back up a bit. What are you talking about?"

Rochelle brought her up to speed. "Let me do some digging. Don't worry, I'll be discreet. I think you might need to find yourself a medium. I'm more concerned with the reaper's statement that something is interfering with Destiny's wishes. She is a deity you don't want to mess with."

"Amen to that, sister," Rochelle responded. "So what do I do about the phantasm in the meantime?"

"See if Tianna can make a connection."

"She is attempting to contact the reaper."

"She might need to be the one to contact your phantasm."

"The reaper says I will need to do the heavy lifting myself. Tianna's involvement could upset Destiny's plans further."

"What happens if you don't deal with this issue?"

"The end of the world."

"Huh!" There was silence on Sophia's end for a few seconds as she digested the information. "Let's save the world now and worry about the rest later."

"Good idea," Rochelle said.

"Talk to you soon," Sophia stated before hanging up.

After checking the coast was still clear, Tianna made her way back to Rochelle. "I can't get a hold of him."

"That's okay, Tianna. Is Cameron still over there?"

Tianna glanced over her shoulder. "Yes."

"See if you can connect with him."

"You want me to break the rules and show myself to a human?"

"No, but we don't have a choice. Besides, he is not really a human at the moment. He is a phantasm. I need you to try to talk to him."

Tianna flew towards Cameron, slowing down as his eyes began to widen. *"Don't be afraid. I won't hurt you."*

Cameron blinked a few times before rubbing his eyes with his fingers. When he took them away, he discovered she was still there. He stared at her, curiosity burning through him. After giving him time to process her existence, she said, *"Do you understand me?"*

Cameron nodded his head, peering behind her to make sure Rochelle had not entered inside his personal space boundary. He noticed she had advanced a few steps but he was happy to stay where he was as long as she remained in that spot. "You tell your friend not to come any closer."

"Her name is Rochelle, and she is here to help you."

"I don't need any help," he said with a confused tone. "Are you a fairy?"

Tianna nodded, *"Are you aware you that you are in spirit form?"*

"Don't be ridiculous," he scoffed. "I am perfectly fine." He frowned and tapped his finger against his lips. "I can't be fine if I believe I am conversing with a fairy."

"We are real entities, Cameron, but we like to keep our existence secret from humans."

"Why is that?"

"For several reasons that are not important at the moment. You are in danger of dying."

"You said that you weren't going to hurt me, then tell me my life is in danger? So you lied to me. Why would you do that?"

"I have not lied to you." She fluttered closer as he took a step back.

"Tell her to stop," his essence began to fade.

"Stop," she yelled, spinning around with a raised hand. *"You're scaring him off."*

She turned back to Cameron and he had disappeared. She searched for him and located him in Keely's room. She and Rochelle high-tailed it inside.

Tianna returned her attention to Cameron, *"Stay and talk to me, Cameron. Go ahead and touch me."*

He reached out his finger to place it against her outstretched hand and gasped when it went straight through. "I don't understand," he said.

"Do you remember being involved in an accident?"

"No," he stated.

"What about afterwards? Can you recall being taken to the hospital?"

"No," he shook his head.

Rochelle's phone rang and, glancing at the screen, she saw the call was from April.

"Hi, April."

"Hi, Rochelle, I'm sorry but I have some bad news for you."

When Cameron spotted the reaper standing beside Tianna, anger crossed his face moments before he disappeared. Tianna spluttered with surprise. *"Cameron,"* she called. Spinning around to let Rochelle know he was gone.

"Oh damn it; the blasted thing has gone to the ghostly plane," exclaimed Rochelle.

"Rochelle, this is important. I need your full, undivided attention. Can you do that?" She caught the serious tone to April's voice and sat on the edge of the bed.

"Okay, April. Sorry, I'm listening."

April then told her the saga of Toren taking the lead in tracking down the vampire queen, Sarina, but had been involved in a helicopter accident and was seriously injured. "To stop humans finding out about the Battle Stars, he has been taken to the planet, Mystique, to be healed."

"Thanks for telling me, April. Please let me know as soon as he returns," she said, concluding the call.

Tianna saw Wang Cho standing beside her. "Great," she threw her hands in the air. "Now, he is going to associate her with you. What were you thinking?"

Rochelle raised an eyebrow. "What's going on?"

"*You* called *me*," the reaper said, getting all high and mighty.

Tianna blew out a breath, her fringe rising and falling on the breeze. *"Cameron disappeared, as soon as he saw him."*

"Who?" Rochelle almost yelled with frustration and worry over Toren.

"The reaper," Tianna said.

"The reaper is here?" Rochelle gulped.

"Standing right beside you."

Swear words swirled inside her head. "Can you ask him why I can't see Cameron?"

"He can hear you, Rochelle."

Tianna looked at him expectantly. When he didn't respond, she said, "You going to answer her question?"

"Is she, or is she not, a Battle Star?" he cleared his throat before qualifying, "a Gatherer?"

Tianna rolled her eyes. "Stating the obvious is not an answer."

"She needs to work it out herself. I cannot interfere any further. I have already told you this."

"Wait," Tianna held up her hand out of fear that he too would leave. "She can't see him. You said she would be able to see him. Answer the question."

"Can she or can she not transform herself?"

"Are you going to answer the damned question or not?" She threw her hands in the air, then began kicking her legs. When he raised an eyebrow, she grabbed the spear from her belt and pointed it at him. "I might be little, but I'm not afraid to use this," she growled.

Wang Cho managed a straight face for a couple of seconds before throwing his head back and laughing like a crazy person. When she jabbed him in the neck with the spear, his laughter died to a loud chuckle with a couple of hiccoughs thrown in. "Not nice," he said, then vanished.

Tianna kicked her leg like a bull about to charge a matador. Her fist waved the spear in the air. Rochelle became quite concerned. "It's not worth it," she told the fairy. "Tell him to get lost."

"He's already gone," she scowled.

"Did he say anything before he left?"

"He asked if you were a Gatherer and if you could transform."

Rochelle left the house and walked towards her car. She needed time to think. The phantasm had gone to the ghostly plane and could take several days to reappear so she had plenty of time. Sliding into the driver's seat, she drummed her fingers on the steering wheel. "Where's a good place to think, T?"

Tianna raised her eyebrows in surprise. Nobody had ever shortened her name before. *"Do you prefer quiet, or background noise?"* she queried.

"Quiet, when I need to sort through stuff."

"Why don't you head out to the dam? It's a beautiful environment that is big enough to find an area free from other individuals."

"That is a great idea," Rochelle grinned, putting her destination into the navigator. By the time they arrived twenty minutes later, her brain had already formulated a plan. She had come up with two options. Pulling into a car park, she encouraged Tianna to take a seat on her shoulder. Walking to the water's edge, she said, "So, I've been thinking about what the reaper asked, and I think I know what he was getting at. He wanted to know if I could morph my body into another shape. Perhaps to be able to see Cameron, I need to become something else."

"Yes, that makes sense," Tianna nodded. "Have you come up with a creature that may be able to see lost souls?"

"Yes. You can see and hear Cameron. Why don't I transform into a fairy?"

"Won't work, Rochelle. Even though you will be tiny like me and look similar to me, you will not be a supernatural being. It is the magical part of me that makes it possible for me to see phantasms. Sorry."

"Damn. Okay. My second thought was a cat. Unfortunately, those two ideas struck such a chord with me, I couldn't think of anything else."

"You sound as though that's an issue," Tianna frowned.

"If I still can't see him, I don't know if I can come up with another solution. If I can see him, I don't know how I am going to communicate with him in feline form."

"What do you mean? Does your mind-link only work in human form?"

"Nooooo," Rochelle sighed. "But the connections in the brain for each animal works differently, and it takes time to understand the communication pathways required to connect to another species. Time, which I may not have."

"So, let's practise now, shall we?"

Rochelle glanced around to see if there were any humans in the vicinity. Not seeing any within range, she transformed herself into a tabby and fought the instinct to launch herself at Tianna, who was fluttering dangerously close. Rochelle tried to send her a message to keep her distance, but Tianna remained where she was. Within killing range.

Perhaps she thought her magic would save her. She was wrong. Maybe she figured she was safe because Rochelle was a Gatherer. Bzzzz! Also wrong. Rochelle was fighting extremely hard to control her feline instincts and quickly realised she could not do both. She would have to give her complete concentration to the task of discovering the communication pathways to mind-linking as a cat or transform herself into human form to avoid attacking Tianna.

Although the fate of thousands of worlds rested on her ability to connect with Cameron's soul and convince him to return to his body, she couldn't contemplate the thought of murdering a Locator Fairy. That being the case, it was not surprising to see her standing once again in human form.

Tianna scowled at Rochelle. *"What are you doing?"*

"Trying not to kill you," Rochelle growled. "Do you have any idea how tasty you look flapping in front of my face?"

"You wanted to eat me?" she asked incredulously. *"You could have told me that earlier in the day. I could have found somebody else to hunt down the phantasm for you."*

Rochelle rolled her eyes, "When I am in cat form, you look incredibly delicious and fun to play with. When I am in human form, you look like a tiny warrior, more than capable of doing your job."

"Oh, right!" Tianna stated, crossing her arms defensively. *"How was I to know you would see me like that? And you rolled your eyes at me again!"*

"Touché, but you owed me that one as I didn't do it last time you accused me." Rochelle rubbed her hand across her forehead, as though her head hurt. "How have you survived this long?"

"I don't trust normal cats," Tianna huffed, *"but I thought you would be different."*

"For future reference, we still maintain our ability to focus on the requirements of the job, but our instincts become the same as the animal we transform into."

"Good to know. Do you want to try again?" At Rochelle's nod, she said, *"Just give me a couple of minutes to hide."*

Tianna took refuge in a nearby bush and prayed the Rochelle cat would keep her mind on the job. She waited nervously for Rochelle's transformation, prepared to take flight at the first indication that the cat wanted to hunt her instead of apparitions that may be lurking in the area. She breathed a sigh of relief when the feline inspected her immediate surroundings then focussed her attention in the opposite direction. Tianna felt a flutter of excitement in her chest that the experiment was working and she had discovered the presence of a ghost. Her joy was short-lived when a Maltese-cross suddenly appeared over the rise with its owner nowhere to be seen.

Rochelle cat hissed, her back arched in warning as the dog bounded towards her eagerly. Tianna's hands flew to her mouth as she pictured the dog taking the cat by the scruff of her neck and shaking her to death. Rochelle bounced sideways, her hissing increasing in volume as the dog finally slowed its pace. The dog barked once as it lowered its front legs and wagged its tail rapidly. Rochelle didn't take long to find the connections that would allow her to communicate with the dog.

She had often taken the form of a large dog when hunting creatures in crowded public places. Cats, she had found, held an abundance of information. Always positioning themselves in a place from which they could study the behaviours of those around them. Reversing the process of communication between dog and cat turned out to be a piece of cake. Rochelle was holding a discussion with the dog through mind-link in no time.

"Slow down there, buddy. You might find yourself not liking the consequences of your actions if you continue rushing at me."

"How did you know my name?" the dog asked. *"Have we met before?"*

"Lucky guess," Rochelle answered, then lifted her paw and licked it a couple of times. The dog watched the action and wiggled its rear. *"Don't even think about it!"* she warned.

The dog sat on its haunches and huffed. *"I wasn't going to do anything,"* he said unconvincingly.

"How old are you?" Rochelle asked.

"I don't know," the dog peered over its shoulder.

"Where is your owner?"

"Coming."

"You'd best go find them," Rochelle advised. *"I'm busy."*

"Doing what?"

"Looking for a phantasm."

The dog burst into laughter. He flopped onto his back and rocked from side to side. Rochelle narrowed her eyes. She thought about launching herself at the dog and biting one of the paws that flailed around in the air. Instead, she asked, *"What's so funny?"*

"Cats can't see the deceased."

"Says who?"

"Every cat I've ever had the misfortune of having to listen to while trapped in my backyard."

Rochelle gave him a puzzled look.

"When I used to become super cranky at them sitting on the fence and goading me with their taunts, they would pretend I had a ghost standing behind me. They would laugh at me when I became spooked and tell me I was as stupid as the humans they tricked when they wanted to be left alone."

"What do you mean?" Rochelle asked, seeking further clarification.

"Cats prefer to be on their own. They will seek out human company, but only on their own terms. If they really want to be left alone, they will focus on a spot and hiss as though something is there. Apparently, the humans freak out with the majority of them fleeing the room."

"Well, lucky for me. A phantasm is not from a deceased body. His spirit has been separated from his body which is still alive," Rochelle smiled at Buddy.

"Doesn't matter. Cats still can't see 'spirits.'" Buddy was thoroughly enjoying upsetting the cat. It didn't happen very often.

Rochelle lay on her belly, feeling quite deflated. She had pinned most of her hopes on the feline form being able to see what she couldn't. As she had told

Tianna earlier, her mind had fixated on this being the answer to making a connection with Cameron. Now that this had been quashed, she had no idea what to do next.

For the first time ever, Rochelle was at a loss. She wished she could discuss the situation with Toren. This mission was supposed to be a level five. No big deal and quick to resolve. The last thing she needed was for him to think she was incompetent. He had enough on his plate with the helicopter accident and the vampire, Sarina, to capture, without having to worry about her, too.

The dog's owner came running towards them. She was a young girl, about eleven years of age. Her ponytail swung to the same rhythm as the lead that hung from her hands. "Come here, you naughty boy."

Buddy walked towards his owner with his belly scraping along the ground. *"Good luck with your ghost,"* he barked over his shoulder.

A couple of days later, Rochelle returned to Keely's room to see if he had returned. She began muttering to herself in frustration because she still couldn't see the phantasm so didn't know if he was there or not.

From outside, she heard a voice saying, "Rochelle, it's Guardians Elden and Manuel. May we come in?"

She poked her head out the window and told them she would come out to them. They related what had happened to Toren. He was on the planet, Mystique, after having been bitten by Sarina and turned into a vampire. She would never be able to discuss this case or anything else with him ever again. She would never feel his loving arms around her. Never feel his lips on hers. Never spend private time with him. When Guardian Elden handed her the little box containing an engagement ring that Queen Adair had been tasked by Toren to pass on to her, that was when her whole life imploded.

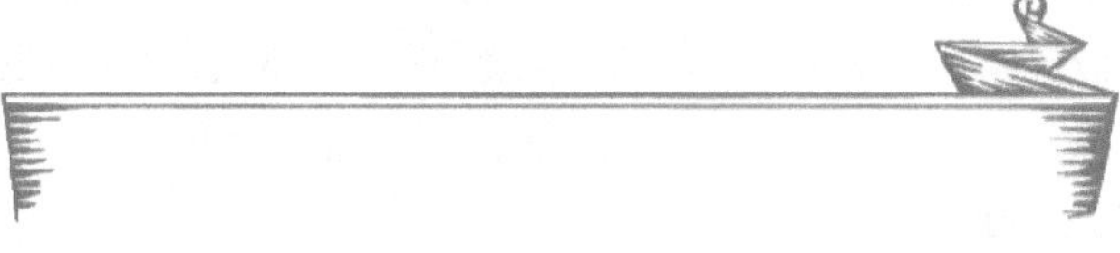
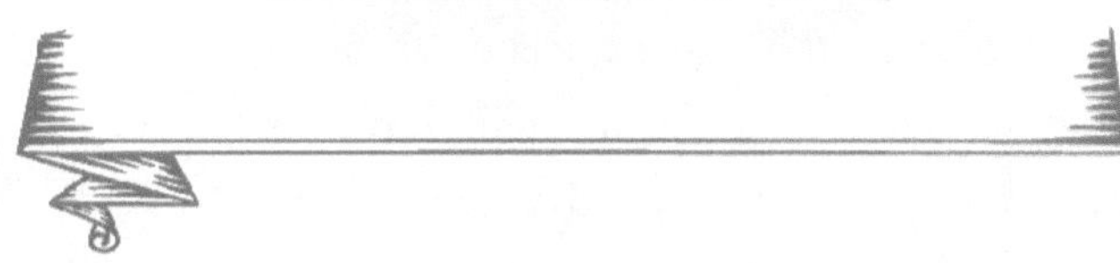

Seventeen

The transfer of images through mind-link ceased. Chandra rubbed her hand across her forehead. No wonder Rochelle had lost it and caused such havoc with the weather. Unfortunately, there was no time to dwell on Toren's misfortune now. If they didn't concentrate on saving Cameron, the whole world was in trouble. So, getting back to Cameron, Rochelle could hardly expect to create a relationship with him if the two of them weren't in the same vicinity. Instead, she chose to focus the discussion around Cameron's dilemma.

"What his family must be going through." Chandra shook her head in dismay. "How could Cameron do that to them?"

"I don't know. I'm not sure what he hopes to achieve."

"After what you have shown me, I would have to agree with Tianna. Your best chance of getting Cameron to return to his body lies with Keeley. They definitely have a profound connection to one another."

"She is three-years-old, Chandra."

"Yes, but don't rule her out just yet. Let's talk about Karen. The reaper said he sent her a vision showing what our future will look like if he dies. Surely, if that were the case, she would be encouraging him at every opportunity to come back to her. That is what you would do if Toren were lying in a hospital bed unconscious." The words spilled from her mouth before she thought about what she was going to say. Chandra could have kicked herself for being so thoughtless.

She was surprised when the cogs of Rochelle's mind began turning. She could see that Rochelle had put herself in Karen's shoes and determined the mother was behaving unexpectedly. Rochelle said, "The only mention of a vision I have been able to ascertain, other than Cameron's accident, is the one pertaining to the kidnapping of Keeley."

"Did you get a chance to take a peek at Karen's vision?"

"Yes, but it didn't make sense," Rochelle replied. "It appears that Keeley will be kidnapped by some unsavoury people, but I have no idea when. If that is what Cameron is waiting for, he will die before the event occurs. If I can't get him to reconnect in the next couple of days, his soul will be reaped.

"Portals will be torn open, flooding the universes with the evil that has been locked away for hundreds of thousands of years. Life as we know it will come to an end."

Chandra squeezed her lips together. The desire to make a comment about Rochelle's pessimism was on the tip of her tongue. Considering she merely spoke the truth and that it was the wrong time to be pointing this out to her after having just lost the love of her life, she left the comment unsaid. What Rochelle needed right then was the support of a loving sister and a fresh perspective on the situation before them. "Do you mind sharing Karen's vision with me?"

Rochelle shrugged her shoulders. It couldn't hurt. She closed her eyes and examined each of the memories she had created during her visits to the hospital. She held up one for closer inspection then opened her eyes and shared the recollection with her sister.

Rochelle stood beside Karen, discussing the different aspects of being a physiotherapist. Karen appeared to be at ease in Rochelle's company, none of the turmoil she must be feeling reflected on her face. When there was a lull in the conversation, Rochelle waited to see if Karen had anything she wanted to get off her chest. When she remained silent, Rochelle said, "Your daughter tells me you have visions of the future. What is that like?"

Karen flinched slightly, the question was clearly unexpected.

"I'm surprised she told you that."

"Your daughter seems to be quite proud of you if not a little unsettled by it."

Karen nodded her head. "She knows they are usually correct and is a little concerned for her own daughter."

"Why is that?" Rochelle placed her hand on the woman's shoulder. Karen allowed the contact, even though she didn't invite Rochelle to sit. Rochelle allowed her hand to fall, afraid of making Karen feel uncomfortable.

A small smile lifted at the corners of Rochelle's mouth as Karen began to speak, "The latest vision was about Keeley, and it has us a little on edge."

Rochelle nodded her head in understanding, not pushing for more details. She had accomplished her mission and brought the memory to the surface of Karen's brain. Rochelle would be able to get in and out with the woman barely noticing her presence.

They found themselves in the middle of a hallway at the hospital. Johnathon was sitting on a chair outside Cameron's room with Keeley sitting on his lap. Both of them were asleep. A young woman with long brown hair wearing a nurse's uniform walked up to Johnathon and gently woke him.

"Hi, Johnathon. My name is Tanya. I am a friend of Melissa. We are doing our practicum together at the hospital." He smiled at her in that not-quite-awake way of those that have had their nap interrupted. "Melissa has to stay back for another hour and has asked me to collect Keeley from you so that you can go and sit with Cameron."

"That's not necessary," he said, his voice gruff from sleep.

"It's no trouble," she smiled sweetly, reaching forward to scoop Keeley up into her arms.

He rose stiffly from the chair and stretched his weary body. He gave Keeley a kiss on the forehead then wandered slowly towards Cameron's room. The woman hurried away with the sleeping child snuggled tightly against her body. The trip to Keeley's temporary prison was not shown in the vision. The next time they saw her, she was being carried through the inside of a building that resembled an empty warehouse or shed.

The woman had her arm wrapped securely around Keeley's waist, and a hand planted forcefully over Keeley's mouth. Although Keeley struggled desperately to be free, the woman appeared unaffected by the violence of her kicks and punches. The woman strode purposely forward, stepping through a doorway into another section of the building. In the middle of the floor sat a fold-up camp chair and a small square table with a piece of cloth, a pair of scissors, and a bunch of zip ties on its surface.

The woman shoved Keeley into the chair, "Stay still!"

Keeley refused the instruction and launched herself to her feet. The woman grabbed her again and shoved her into the chair harder, tipping it backwards and scaring the child into immobility. The woman swiftly secured her wrists to the armrests and then received a kick to the head as she tied the other leg to the chair leg. "Watch it, kiddo," the woman said briskly.

Chandra leaned closer to Rochelle as she caught a glint in the child's eyes. She was about to say something when the woman glanced at a clock on the wall. Chandra took a deep breath as the numbers were revealed. They were back to front and the hands were moving in an anti-clockwise direction.

"Rochelle," she cried, rousing her from the mind-link.

Rochelle gazed at her with comprehension.

They said unanimously, "The vision is a fake."

They both laughed with relief. "So, you've seen this before?" Chandra asked.

"Not exactly. I have heard of some humans that exhibit powers of persuasion. One of those could have planted the idea in Karen's head, making her think she had seen a vision instead of being told an imaginary story."

Chandra shook her head, "I think it is more than that. I came across a coven of witches a few centuries ago that could construct a false reality. The only way I knew that something wasn't right was a niggling feeling in the pit of my stomach. It took me weeks to realise the water in the sink was moving in the wrong direction when it emptied down the drain. I believe we are dealing with a bunch of witches who are trying to accomplish God-knows-what by Cameron meeting an untimely demise."

"Are you sure?"

"Definitely. Did you notice anything peculiar about Keeley?"

"Should I have?" Rochelle frowned.

"She had the same glint in her eye that a Gatherer has when exposed to purple light."

"A reflection from the woman's eye? How would the woman gain access to that?"

"You are a bit slow, Rochelle."

"Do you think the woman in the vision was one of us?"

"Definitely."

"How could that be?"

"I believe we must take it upon our future selves to force Cameron into saving Keeley's life. We must have come to the conclusion that when he realises he can't manipulate objects in the physical world, he will return to his body to sound the alarm."

"That is ridiculous. Cameron would never leave her at the mercy of a stranger intent on harming her."

"He might if he felt that was the only way to save her. Cameron would know where she was and would be able to tell somebody if he were back in his own body."

Rochelle was flabbergasted, wondering why she hadn't picked up on the clues provided earlier. She jumped to her feet and began to pace. Chandra got up and made them a cup of coffee. Her stomach rumbled, making them both laugh. Rochelle peered inside the cold box and pulled out a loaf of bread, a packet of bacon and a carton of eggs. "This is more in line with breakfast food here, but how about a bacon and egg sandwich?"

"Sounds good to me. Got any sauce?"

Rochelle searched the cupboards, "Tomato or barbecue?"

"Barbecue is good."

"What about the vision the reaper said he sent regarding telling Karen the consequences of Cameron dying? I've seen no evidence of that. Only the brief message that caused Karen to contact Candice."

"I think the witches hijacked his and planted one of their own," Chandra remarked.

"How would they know he would send one?"

"I don't think they did. I think it was a matter of poor timing on Wang's behalf. They probably had the same idea at the same time."

"You don't think they can time-travel do you?"

"Lord, I hope not," Chandra replied with a horrified expression.

"What is our next step?"

Chandra considered their options carefully. "I think a trip to the hospital is in order."

"What do we hope to accomplish there?"

"We are going to turn Cameron's life support off."

Rochelle couldn't believe her ears, "What did you just say?"

"You heard me," Chandra said, unwilling to repeat herself.

"We are not going to turn off his life support."

"Yes. We. Are," Chandra enunciated slowly.

"Over my dead body," Tianna projected her thoughts as she fluttered in through a window.

Chandra swatted the air in front of her to prevent the fairy from getting too close to her face. She had to admit the fairy appeared well and truly ready for battle. Gone was the green pants suit to be replaced by the outfit she was wearing when the reaper came to visit. She had a lovely figure that was shown to perfection in her low cut top and short skirt. A helmet sat securely on her head, and a spear was clutched tightly in her hands, which was currently pointed towards Chandra's head. Her boots were stylish and had a wicked heel that could do a lot of damage to the unsuspecting.

"You can't come in at the end of a conversation and butt in as if you know what is going on," Chandra complained.

"I take it Rochelle has been privy to your entire conversation and is most certainly in agreement with me, not you. Who are you, anyway?" She jabbed the spear at Chandra to accentuate her point.

"I am Chandra, Rochelle's sister. We haven't seen each other for three millennia. Long story of how I came to be here. But I'm going to help her with this phantasm. We are not really going to turn off the machine, Tianna," Chandra explained. "It is a simple yet effective strategy to force Cameron to have contact with us. Once we have been touched by his soul, we will be able to recognise his energy with our own and the communication lines will be opened between us as the reaper wanted."

"What happens then?" Tianna queried, lowering the weapon to her side.

"That depends on Cameron. I have a feeling he is going to reject the truth, and we will be forced to carry out the scenario in Karen's vision."

"You will really pretend to kidnap that little girl?" having picked up the gist of the vision through mind-link as she was approaching the cottage.

"I'm pretty sure that is what will happen, or else the witches would not have been able to use those images to scare Cameron into remaining on his current path through Karen's vision."

"I have to say your logic is impeccable," Rochelle admitted approvingly.

"I've been doing this job as long as you, Sis. You tend to pick up a lot of skills along the way."

"Yes, but I missed so many things on this mission."

"You live in a country where the population is tiny. As a result, the threats to the people here are a lot smaller than where I come from. I have merely been exposed to a higher number of creatures than you probably have. It's no big deal. Besides you have been worried about your man, and with good reason. It had to be hard to keep your mind fully focused on the job when your fella was in danger."

Rochelle didn't say anything. She didn't have to.

Chandra quietened her tone, "We can wait until tomorrow if you like. The world won't end overnight."

"You don't know that," Rochelle sighed. "Besides, it will be easier in the earlier hours of the morning to try your idea. The family aren't allowed to stay past ten, and they won't be back before eight. That will give us ten hours to try to coax Cameron back to the living without having to invoke a fake kidnapping."

Tianna flew to the middle of the table and landed on the rim of a flowerpot. She sniffed deeply, scowling crossly as the only scent that reached her nose was the hot drinks and greasy sandwiches.

Rochelle laughed. "They are fake, Tianna. Toren was meant to surprise me with a bunch of fresh flowers on our anniversary. Unfortunately, he was bitten by a vampire and taken to Mystique."

"Oh, so that was what Chandra was talking about. I am so sorry," she said, landing on Rochelle's shoulder and huddling against her neck. She spread her arms across the surface and moved them as though making a snow angel on Rochelle's skin. The action tickled, and Rochelle only just managed to stop herself from swatting Tianna away like an annoying bug.

"Thank you," Rochelle said. "I love your fairy hugs." *Even though they tickle like crazy.*

"Is that why you were crying outside the house when those men came?"

"You saw that?"

"Hmm, hmm. I didn't stay because I needed to find shelter from the approaching storm," Tianna murmured.

"Yeah, the guardians had just informed me of Toren's plight. I don't want to talk about it, or I will start crying again."

"That's okay," Tianna said, returning to the flowerpot. She sat on the edge with her legs crossed at the knees. "*Eat your dinner, and we will find something to do until it is time to return to the hospital.*"

"I'm glad you are here, Tianna. I was worried about you." *The thought of you never crossed my mind.*

"*I heard that,*" Tianna scowled. "*But you are forgiven. You've had a lot on your plate. Fancy seeing your sister after all this time.*"

"Yeah," Rochelle said with her first genuine smile of the evening. "Thank goodness for small blessings."

"I hope you still feel that way when I anger our spirit boy."

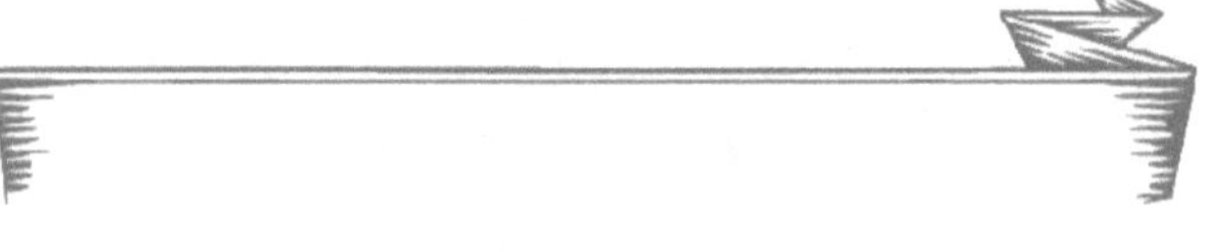

Eighteen

Feeling fairly sure that they would not be back for many hours and it would be impossible to sneak it at the hospital without being seen, Rochelle decided to drink the required glass of water containing the pinch of fairy dust given to her by Guardian Elden. He had stressed that she must take it every night with a glass of water, without fail, if she was going to be able to save Toren. She would do anything to save him, no matter how inconvenient.

The sisters arrived at the hospital during the change of shift. Like last time, Tianna tucked her body inside Rochelle's bun, and the girls transformed their outfits to blend in with the other staff. Rochelle led Chandra directly to Cameron's room using her mind-control abilities to ensure their progress was not delayed.

Once they entered the room, they listened intently as the nurse-on-duty gave them a rundown of Cameron's vitals over the past eight hours. They took up their respective positions at the head and foot of the bed. Chandra worried that the nurse would question the need for both of them to be in the room. Rochelle had met the woman earlier, and she was well aware that Rochelle was not an Intensive Care professional.

Chandra breathed a sigh of relief when they were alone again. Tianna came out of hiding and surveyed the room. *"His spirit is not present,"* she confirmed for their benefit.

"Let's see if we can get him to make an appearance shall we," said Chandra, moving towards the switch.

Tianna's body shuddered as though she were being electrocuted. The Gatherers raced to the middle of the bed and watched her with horror. A high pitched squeal erupted from her as the violence of movement increased. Rochelle searched the room for the source of energy while Chandra attempted to deflect the current away.

Tianna's convulsions stopped as suddenly as they'd begun, her body falling swiftly towards the bed. Rochelle sent a cushion of air sprawling beneath her to soften the fall. The fairy landed face down, the spearhead barely missing her ribcage. Chandra slid the weapon free from her body before carefully turning her over. She raised her eyes to Rochelle's, to find the same level of concern reflected there.

"Her breathing is quite shallow. Should we send her some healing energy?"

"Just give it a minute. If she stops breathing or her heart stops beating, then we'll have to do something."

"What the hell happened to her?"

"I don't know."

"There's been no change with Cameron."

"Did you expect there to be?"

"No, not really. It's a bit strange that it started happening right after you said you were going to turn off the machine."

"Do you think he is here?"

"No. Melissa felt a chill whenever Cameron was in the vicinity. We would too."

Tianna groaned. Her hand moved slowly towards her head.

"You alright, T?" Rochelle asked softly.

"*No,*" Tianna groaned. "*That hurt. A lot.*" She opened her eyes slowly and stared at the ceiling. "*Why am I the one that cops it all the time?*"

"I'm sorry little one," a male voice murmured. "You were my only chance of stopping Chandra from touching that button."

Tianna turned her head to the side, "Figures, it would be you."

"Who is it, Tianna?"

"Wang Cho, the reaper," she said. "How could you be so cruel?"

"It didn't hurt," he lifted his chin defiantly.

"Wanna bet?"

"I don't need to. Are you in pain?"

Tianna inspected her body. Apart from a dull ache in her head, there were no lasting effects from her spasms. "Why did you do that?"

"I told you, I needed Chandra to leave the machine alone."

"Why? What better way to get Cameron to return than to turn the machine off."

"You turn that machine off, and you will kill him for good."

"What do you mean?" Tianna asked, scrambling to her feet.

"Trust me on this," he replied, moving to the head of the bed. He placed his hand on Cameron's chest and closed his eyes. When he opened them, they were troubled. "I can feel them, the ones who caused this. Their wickedness has enveloped him like a blanket. I feel it pulsing beneath my fingertips, drawing him deeper into their web. Your time is almost up. I cannot hold off for much longer."

"Tell us what to do!" Tianna begged.

Wang regarded her with pity then vanished into thin air. Tianna stamped her foot, *"Dammit, he is gone again."*

"Yes, we know. We tapped into your mind so we could follow along."

"No wonder my head hurt with the both of you in there."

"It probably had more to do with him shocking you, don't you think?" Rochelle asked.

"Nah, it's true what he said. It might have looked shocking, but it didn't hurt at all once he stopped. It was just the surprise of it all that knocked me out for a bit."

"What do we do now?" asked Chandra.

"I don't know," Rochelle replied. "We come up with something else. Chandra, why don't you try to get a reading off him?"

Chandra moved forward and unknowingly placed her hand over the spot Wang Cho had vacated. She shuddered violently as sensations threatened to overwhelm her. Rochelle and Tianna worried that Wang Cho was at it again. Chandra opened her mind to allow the girls to connect with what she saw and felt.

A swirling mass of vapours clamoured over Cameron's body. The emptiness in Cameron's mind was unfamiliar and disturbing. Even in unconsciousness, the brain worked tirelessly creating one dream after another. That was not the case with Cameron. Beneath Chandra's hand was proof that there was nothing natural about this case. A small thread of essence belonging to the reaper remained behind. Chandra narrowed her eyes as she concentrated her focus on the remnants of his energy. "He is going after Cameron."

"For what purpose?" Rochelle asked.

"I'm not sure."

"I hope it's not to reap his soul," Tianna sniffled.

Chandra said, "The reaper said there was still a small window of opportunity to save him. I think it is time we put our kidnapping proposal into action."

"That is not going to help if Cameron is not around to see it happen. How are we ever going to find him?"

"He will be wherever Keeley is located. His determination to save her will ensure he is never far away. We should make our way to her place. Hopefully, by the time we get there, Melissa will be asleep, and we can sneak in and "attempt" to snatch Keeley."

Rochelle played-out the scenario in her head, "He will try to stop us, creating an energy link with us. From there, we will be able to pinpoint his energy signature, allowing us to bond with him."

"Exactly," Chandra grinned. "We will be able to see and talk to him like any other person."

Wang Cho moved from the hospital room to Keeley's bedroom in a blink of an eye. He knew he would find Cameron's soul lurking somewhere nearby, but was unable to pinpoint its whereabouts with absolute accuracy. The further Cameron distanced himself from the living world, the more influential the entity controlling him became.

It took the reaper a few minutes to locate his position. He found him in the garage, lying dormant inside the boot of Melissa's car. Not wanting to be confined to such a small area, Wang popped the lid and used his powers to prevent Cameron from moving outside of their current plane.

"Hello, Cameron," he said gently. "I'm a bit surprised to see you here."

"Why?" Cameron asked, clearly confused.

"I thought you would be watching over Keeley."

"I should be?"

"How long have you been in here Cameron?"

"I'm not sure," Cameron admitted. "Since the last time Melissa drove home from the hospital. They seem to feel cold when they are around me so I travel in the boot."

"And when was that?"

"Not long ago," he frowned trying to remember.

"Where have you been lately?"

"Um, the hospital." He grappled with his rising frustration knowing that would only hinder his ability to think. "I remember being at the intersection where Melissa lives, Keeley's bedroom, and I think I spoke to a fairy a couple of times," he finished excitedly.

"That is great, Cameron. I'm pleased to hear you haven't been stuck in here all this time."

"You are?"

"Yes, but now I need you to come with me."

"Where?" Cameron queried, not sure he wanted to go anywhere with the man in the suit.

"To the hospital. It appears that a couple of nurses are discussing the possibility of turning off your life support system."

"My life support system?"

Wang sighed, moving to perch himself on the edge of the boot. "Your body in the hospital is taking up the spot of somebody who requires the equipment housed there to survive," the reaper lied. "There is no medical reason for you to be in a prolonged coma since they stopped giving you the medication that placed you in the coma. While your injuries are quite severe, they do not equate to your body's inability to awaken. The current consensus among the medical staff is that you should be taken off life support to see if you are capable of surviving on your own."

"So?" Cameron replied, finally remembering his situation. "Let them do whatever they think needs to be done."

"You will not survive it, Cameron. Your soul and body are separated. Your body cannot live on its own without the soul. I will have to reap your soul, and you will not be able to complete your mission. You must go to the hospital to stop the nurses from turning off the machines."

"I cannot go there," he shook his head. "I have something vital to do here."

"What? Lying in the boot of a car? What do you have to do that is more important than saving your life, Cameron?"

Cameron frowned. "Just give me a moment to remember."

"You are quickly running out of moments, Cameron. You are almost at the end of your rope. Once you reach the end, it is a long drop to a place you are not ready to enter."

Cameron sat up quickly, "Are you saying I am destined for Hell?"

"No, of course not."

"But you just said I have a long drop . . ."

"That is not what I meant," Wang assured him. "Cameron, you must go back to the hospital. I insist." He grabbed Cameron by the arm and whisked him away. Regret sat heavily on his heart as he was reduced to forcing his will on the boy. *Desperate times call for desperate measures.*

They arrived at the hospital to discover the trio had left the room. The reaper cursed beneath his breath and dragged an uncooperative Cameron through the hallways. They found the sisters exiting the elevator on the ground floor. Tianna was the only one who could see them, and she was currently plastered against Rochelle's head, pretending to be a hair accessory.

"Fairy," the reaper called.

Tianna sprang forward, her thoughts shouting at the Gatherers to pay attention. *"The reaper is here with Cameron."*

The Gatherers stopped in their tracks, "Where are they?"

"Right beside you, to the left."

"What do they want?"

Tianna listened intently. *"He wants us to return to Cameron's room."*

"Why?"

*"He wants us to **check** the machines."*

Rochelle and Chandra turned to one another and spoke through mind-link, *"Are you thinking what I am thinking?"*

Chandra answered, *"I think the reaper wants us to pretend to turn off the machine to see what Cameron will do."*

"Yeah, that was my thought, too."

They waited for the elevator to return and then stepped inside. A chill in the air caused goosebumps to rise on their skin. A good indication Cameron was still with them. Rochelle contemplated moving around the small space to force the bond to form. She tossed the thought aside, realising she might end up linking with the reaper instead. A fate she feared more than death.

There were nurses at the desk that needed to be dealt with. It took a few minutes longer to re-enter the room than they would have liked. They then had to spend time convincing the assigned nurse to vacate the premises until recalled to duty. This was always a time-consuming exercise. In the meantime, Cameron viewed their behaviour suspiciously.

"I don't think you two are real nurses," he grumbled.

"You would be right," Chandra said, being able to hear the phantasm through mind-link with Tianna. Trusting her instincts, she continued, "We are here to make sure you don't interfere with our plans for your niece. She is instrumental to the success of our operation, and we can't have you messing that up for us."

Rochelle, who was closest to the plug, stepped forward and leant towards the floor.

"What are you doing?" Cameron screamed, launching himself forward. His body fell into Rochelle's, then continued on until reaching the floor.

He flipped onto his back and stared at her with raised arms and angry eyes. "Leave it alone," he warned.

Rochelle stood up, shivering from head to toe with a chill that had gone right through to her bones. Looking down, Rochelle could now see Cameron's spirit. "You can't stop me from turning off the machine, Cameron. You are a phantasm with no control over the physical realm. You aren't even competent enough to possess a body. How do you expect to save your niece? I am flesh and blood, you are a gust of air."

Cameron glared at her. She could tell he was processing the information she had given him and was loathed to come to the same conclusion. She gave him a few more minutes and then moved her hand towards the power supply. His body rose through hers once more, giving her a moment's pause. As her finger touched the power switch, his body settled quickly above his body. He lowered himself carefully, finding the entrance blocked by an unseen force. With panic in his eyes, he said, "I can't get in."

Rochelle moved closer to the bed, her attention locked on the shimmering block of energy that constituted Cameron's soul. It hovered millimetres above the blankets, perfectly aligned to the body lying beneath. She gave him words of encouragement that were of no help at all. Everything she suggested ended in failed attempts to merge the two halves together. Cameron slammed his arms down in frustration, rising swiftly into the air. In his panic, he rolled to the side and fell to the floor passing through

Chandra's body. She stumbled backwards as the cold seeped into her skin. Once she got past the chill in her bones, she was pleasantly surprised to discover she could now see him as clearly as Rochelle and Tianna.

The reaper expelled every speck of emotion that resided in his psyche, allowing him to view the scene with a clear perspective. He evaluated events which had transpired over the past few months with a logical efficacy that enabled him to spot any anomalies that had previously gone undetected. His face brightened with the realisation that David's death and Cameron's accident were related.

Tianna noticed the change in him and questioned the cause.

He looked at her with excitement. "This is the last time I can offer my assistance to you all, little fairy. Once you have delivered my latest message to the Gatherers, you must return home and leave the Gatherers to succeed or fail on their own. They are now capable of communicating with Cameron without your assistance. Your role in this mission is over."

"What is the message?" Tianna scowled, not wanting to go home until Cameron was safely returned to his body.

"I told you at the outset that this would be the way of things," he reminded her.

"Yes, I know," she grumbled, pulling the homing device from her satchel. "What do you want me to tell them?"

He straightened his shoulders and puffed out his chest. "David and Cameron are linked together somehow. I believe the witches initially targeted David. He had a terminal illness that would have ended up killing him before year's end anyway. As he was already destined to die within a short space of time, I believe their plan backfired. For whatever reason their focus turned towards Cameron, using him to finish what they'd started with David.

"Tell the Gatherers they either need to figure out what the witches are trying to accomplish by causing a death out of sequence or discover the weapon they used to shorten David's lifespan. Once they have the answers to one of those, I am sure they will be able to thwart the witches' plans. Cameron's soul will be able to reattach to his body, and the opening of portals unleashing evil to many worlds will be averted."

The reaper waited expectantly for Tianna to relay the message. Once she had accomplished the task, he escorted her from the building, ensuring she would be invisible to all present. With her helmet fitted securely to her head, and the spear ensconced tightly in her hand, Tianna followed the directions from her homing device and made it safely to her tree before dawn. She collected a nasturtium flower from the cupboard and drank deeply. Then she climbed into her hammock for a well-earned rest.

Meanwhile, Cameron and the sisters decided to move to a more conducive environment to work out a solution to Cameron's situation. Their departure allowed his nurse to return to monitor his condition, ensuring his body was kept alive.

The sisters chose to take Cameron back to Rochelle's cabin where they could talk amongst themselves in peace. Cameron wanted to ride in the boot. Chandra and Rochelle convinced him to sit in the passenger compartment with them. To keep the interior warmer, Rochelle closed the roof and turned the air conditioning unit to heat.

The ride was long and tedious. Chandra was not willing to engage in conversation in case she forgot to monitor Cameron's energy, and he disappeared from view. Rochelle concentrated on navigating the streets. Though they were becoming more familiar, she had not reached the point where she could talk and drive simultaneously.

Cameron managed to keep his wits about him for the entire journey. He had become despondent to find it was increasingly difficult to keep his mind focused on one thing. Quite often, his thoughts would have him moving from one location to another. Although he always managed to find his way back to Keeley, his lack of mental clarity was quickly becoming a hindrance to his plan. His realisation that there was a way to pin himself to one location uplifted his mood immensely.

They began their investigation at the kitchen table with a cup of coffee and writing implements in hand. A list of people and places in commonality was added to the sheet of paper first. Then their favourite hobbies and methods of travel were covered. Once the records had been exhausted, they realised there were too many items to be investigated. Leaning back in her seat, Rochelle said, "Tell us about him."

"I haven't really talked about him since he died," Cameron confessed. "It hurts too much."

"Please try. I know how you feel. My partner just died a horrific death, and I can't bear to think about it. I wouldn't ask you to go through that kind of pain if I didn't think it could help us work out what is going on."

Cameron turned his head away to collect his thoughts. The last thing he wanted was to feel judged by them. He floated to the wall and stared out the window, thinking about the time he'd first met his brother-in-law.

David pulled up to the campsite, excited to be spending the entire weekend with Melissa. He had enjoyed dining out and going to the movies with her but it wasn't really his thing. Now he looked forward to spending time outside in the fresh air, throwing a line into the water and observing which reaction would be displayed when her hook captured her first fish.

He jumped out of the SUV and strolled happily towards the kitchen tent. It was a bit of a shock when he rounded the corner and peered in through the meshed wall. An older couple and tween boy were seated at the table, smiling and howling with laughter. He concluded he was looking at the significant people in Melissa's life and that she had finally managed to stitch him up.

Gone were the excuses of why he couldn't meet her family. There they were sitting right in front of him. It was time to suck it up and make an impression. How he interacted with them would set the tone for the remainder of the weekend. He placed a friendly smile on his face and stepped further into view. "Well, hello there," he said in a good-natured tone. Seeking out the location of his girl, who stood cheerfully to the side, he said, "It seems you have started the festivities without me."

Melissa gave him a wide grin. Her eyes lit up like candles when she spotted him. She skipped slightly as she made her way towards him. He wrapped his arm around her and gave her a short kiss on the mouth. "Happy anniversary," he whispered.

She gazed at him adoringly, "This is my family. My mother - Karen, my father - Johnathon, and my brother - Cameron. I hope you don't mind, they will be spending the weekend with us." Turning her head towards them, she said, "This is my boyfriend, David."

Johnathon rose to greet him. He held out his hand, "Good to meet you, David. We've heard quite a bit about you."

"Dad," Melissa admonished gaily.

Karen stepped up next and pulled him in for a hug. David beamed at her. Cameron merely waved from his seat, David promptly returning the motion. The rest of the weekend went swimmingly with everyone getting along famously. Cameron and David related to each other like old friends. Their relationship grew more substantially over the following few months. In time, they treated each other like brothers, thick as thieves and pranks galore.

Cameron acted as junior groomsman at their wedding. He was there the night Keeley was born two years later, sitting in the waiting room longing for word that the ordeal was over. He heard screams from down the hallway, though he was unsure if they were coming from his sister or some other poor woman. Their haunting howls were unnatural to his ears. He breathed a sigh of relief when David bounded into view. His face shone with contentment as he held the swaddled baby in his arms. Cameron had never seen the man so happy.

David was a wonderful husband but, in Cameron's view, was an even better father. He took pleasure in teaching Keeley how to fish and ride a bike, which was not surprising considering his love of the outdoors. What did surprise Cameron was the joy David received while lying on the floor with a colouring-in book and pencils, grinning from ear to ear as he argued with Keeley over the colour scheme of their latest masterpiece.

Life had been good. Cameron hadn't become aware of David's sickness until a few days before the accident. He had overheard a conversation between him and Melissa. They were arguing whether they should tell the family he had received a terminal prognosis. David insisted they be given enough time to come to terms with the fact he would most likely die. Melissa wanted to wait until the next visit with his oncologist to see if the treatment was working. When Cameron confronted them, they sat him down and told him the bad news. David had pancreatic cancer. The doctors were not confident he would survive another year, most likely six months.

Cameron ran out of the room before they could stop him. Melissa chased after him, but he was too fast for her to catch him. She had to let him go and trust that he would keep the information to himself. After a few hours fraught with worry, he returned to gather more information. Melissa was able to sit down and talk to him like an adult. When she had said all she could say, Melissa left to give him some time to process the facts in his own time. Not long after, David entered the room.

They chatted for a couple of hours about many things. The most important, as far as David was concerned, was Cameron's willingness to step up as a strong role model for Keeley when the time came. It was not that he didn't feel that Johnathon would do a good job, it was simply that Cameron had more spare time in the afternoons for Keeley, and could have the occasional sleepover.

David admitted how thankful he was for the love and support he received from Melissa's family. He had lost his parents at a young age and grew up in the foster care system. The couple he was placed with saw him through to adulthood. He still had regular contact with them. They came to the wedding and one of his foster brothers was his best man, but David didn't feel as close to them as he did to Melissa's family.

"The last six years have been the best years of my life, Cameron," he had said. "My only regret is not having the opportunity to see my daughter grow up. I won't be there to scare the living daylights out of the first guy brave enough to offer her a kiss. I won't be there when she graduates from high school and university. I won't get to teach her how to drive or give her away at her wedding. And I won't be there to hold my grandchild for the first time." He sighed deeply and closed his eyes.

"Are you okay?" Cameron panicked.

"Yeah," he said quietly. "Just a little tired."

That was the last thing David said to him. He died a few days later, losing his balance on a platform at the train station. He fell onto the tracks of an incoming train and died instantly. Until the reaper had come to his stunning conclusion, Cameron had thought David's death was an unfortunate accident, resulting from the side-effects of his latest treatment. Now it seemed, there was foul play involved, and he was determined to get to the bottom of it.

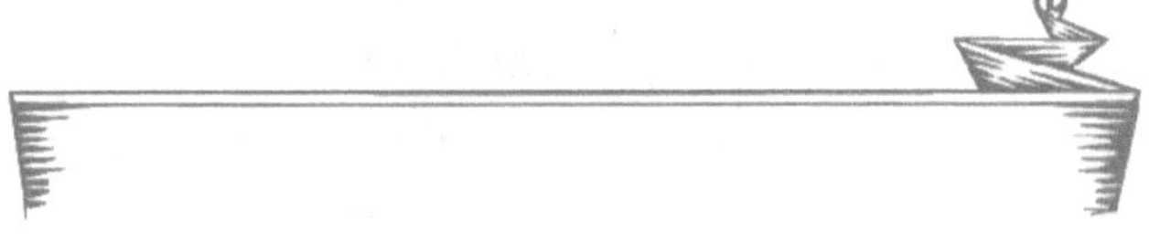

Twenty

Chandra stretched her body, linking her hands together behind her back and raising herself onto her toes. She pushed out with her arms, receiving pleasure from the pulling sensation of her muscles. "I don't understand why witches would have targeted him."

Rochelle turned her head to bring her into view. "He was a young man, full of vitality until he started his new medication. He was also a loving husband and the father of a young girl. Why not target somebody like him to unravel the fabric of the universe?"

"I suppose," Chandra shrugged.

"How would they have gained access to him?" puzzled Cameron.

"That is the million-dollar question," Chandra replied, continuing to lower her body and raise herself to get the blood flowing. "There has to be something that ties the two of you together. Witches are renowned for utilising cursed objects and hex bags to do their dirty work for them."

Rochelle tapped the side of her chin, "Did David leave you anything in his will?"

Cameron's spirit flared brightly, "He left me a necklace with an angel medallion he had found hanging from a low branch of a tree in his front yard. He had handed it in to the police station. After thirty days, they had contacted him to see if he would like to keep it as they were unable to locate its owner. He felt it was a good luck charm and happily took it back. I wonder if it was left there by the witches."

Rochelle asked, "Why did he leave it to you and not Melissa?"

"The setting is too masculine for a woman to wear," he replied.

"Where is it now?" Chandra asked, placing a hand on her hip and lowering her heels.

"I put it on the moment I received it and haven't taken it off since," he said.

Chandra glanced at Rochelle, who shook her head, "It isn't on his body at the hospital. They removed everything when they put him in a hospital gown and took him to surgery."

"Then it must be where his personal effects are. Would they have given his clothes and jewellery back to his parents for cleaning and safekeeping?"

"More than likely," Rochelle agreed.

"We need to go to Cameron's and find that necklace."

"How are we going to get in without waking Mum and Dad? They arm the downstairs alarm when they go to bed."

"Do they sleep with a window open upstairs?" Chandra queried.

"No, they use the air conditioner," he supplied.

"Of course, they do," Rochelle cursed.

Twenty-One

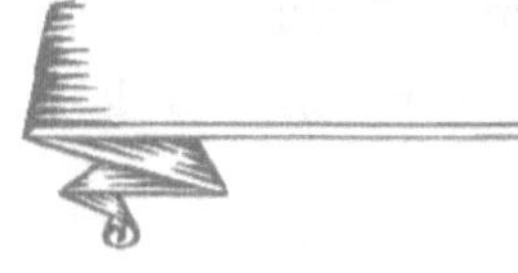

Rochelle contacted the Starlight Investigation team and requested a containment box capable of holding a cursed object. Samuel took the delivery details and assured her it would arrive within forty-eight hours.

Chandra cleared the dishes, her mind working furiously. "I don't think the cursed object is the reason you are locked out of your body, Cameron. There has to be something else at play here."

"Like what?" he asked.

"I don't know. Some kind of hex or spell that the witches have performed."

"Are you sure witches are involved?"

"Most definitely. I'd like to return to the hospital while it is quiet and sweep the room."

"Okay," he replied. "Want me to come?"

"Nah, I think you should travel with Rochelle to help her navigate the inside of your home to limit the chances of waking your parents."

"Good idea," he replied. "You'll let us know if you find anything?"

"You bet," she said.

Rochelle excused herself and entered the bathroom where she took a pinch of the fairy dust given to her by Guardian Elden and ingested it with a glass of water. She walked back into the kitchen and said, "Let's go."

Arriving at Cameron's house, Chandra got out of the car, looked around to make sure no one was watching and transformed herself into a German shepherd.

She ran over footpaths and street crossings, copping a few looks from those who were out and about, but they didn't give her more than a cursory glance. Once the shock of seeing a large dog roaming free wore off, they quickly returned to their respective activities.

Chandra slowed to a stop when she reached the carpark and casually looked around. Not seeing anybody in the vicinity, she transformed back into her own form and boldly moved towards the entrance. The fact that the front doors were locked did not deter her at all. She made her way to Emergency and with the hospital uniform adorning her body, was given passage through the internal doors, which allowed her access to the entire building. Chandra quickly made her way to Intensive Care and stepped inside Cameron's room.

The nurse opened her mouth to protest, but Chandra took care of her concerns swiftly. The woman went back to work as though Chandra wasn't there. Chandra stood against the back wall for a few minutes to allow the room's energy to settle. Then she sent out her psyche and probed the room looking for that which didn't belong. Her search showed up nothing. With a grumbled growl, she decided she would have to do it the old-fashioned way, and set to checking everything in the room with a thorough hand and critical eye.

After thirty minutes, she had come up empty. Chandra looked at the bed and with a determined attitude and a fearless heart began searching his body for a mark left behind by the witches. She started at his neck, the place the cursed necklace had rested for months. There was no sign the chain had ever settled against his skin. Chandra snorted and continued her search.

She peered through the strands of hair and checked inside his ears, nostrils and mouth. The area beneath his chin and behind his ears also showed up nothing. She poured over his chest and down his arms, making sure to search between his fingers. She lowered the sheet and scanned his abdominal area, baulking at the fact she would have to continue lower.

Chandra wished she had gained Cameron's consent to complete a full-body search. The fact that he lay unconscious did nothing to allay her guilt over what she was about to do. She could not leave any part of him unexamined. Chandra lowered the sheet, and with a clinical detachment she didn't know she possessed; she checked every centimetre of the remaining skin on his body, front and back. She pulled the sheet up after carefully returning his body to its original position and sighed frustratedly.

Chandra sat on a chair and rested her head in her hands. She was sure the witches were using something other than the necklace to force the reaper to collect Cameron's soul. She was annoyed she couldn't find it. Fingers tapped impatiently against her skin as she tried to figure out what she had missed. Perhaps the spell was located back at his place. Maybe she would find it at his sister's home. It would explain why he spent so much time there.

The issue she was having was those thoughts didn't make sense with what she had learnt over the past three millennia. For Cameron to be denied access to his body, the spell would have to be extremely potent. Therefore, logic dictated that a spelled item would have to remain close to his body. A cursed item would not be specific enough to separate a body from its soul. Nor would it be capable of keeping the soul from returning, once the person realised they were not in corporeal form.

How the witches knew Cameron had detached his soul from his body was another thought that troubled her deeply. Knowledge of his situation early on would have been critical in the formulation of a strategy to keep him locked out and trapped on the spiritual plane. Who would benefit most from his condition? Nobody that she could think of. Chandra stood slowly, finally admitting defeat. She had no idea what was going on. It was time to leave and resume her search elsewhere. She turned to Cameron and said "I will find it. I promise."

The nurse lifted her head a touch and stepped back slightly, bumping her hip against the bed. A small package hit the floor, capturing Chandra's attention. It must have been dislodged by her turning the body from front to back and back again. She snatched up the tiny sachet, surprised by the enormity of power emanating from the object. "Gotcha," she grinned, racing from the room. Chandra refused to take a closer look until she had exited the building completely. Once outside, she unwrapped the cloth and gazed at the contents in dismay. What she held in her hand was some seriously dark magic. "Holy . . ."

Rochelle glared at the building. Two-storeys high and built like Fort Knox. She hadn't come across a structure yet, that she hadn't been able to gain access to. What she didn't particularly look forward to were the more complex buildings that required compressing her body composition into a far smaller creature. She glanced at Cameron, "I'm going in through the compressor. All going well, I will exit through the first air vent I come across. From there, I will need to go to the second floor to take on human form. See you on the other side?"

Cameron nodded his head. Rochelle disappeared from view as her body morphed into a regular housefly. Cameron remained frozen in place, momentarily shocked by the speed at which she changed form. He shook off his surprise and floated through the dining room wall. He drifted through various walls in his home until he came to the living area, where he found her buzzing beneath the air vent.

"Follow me," he yelled. Cameron headed for the staircase, not waiting to see if she complied. His soul hovered over each stair as he made his ascent. He turned to the right and floated down the hallway, looking over his shoulder to make sure she was there. Rochelle stood behind him, opening the door once his essence had passed through. She stood in his room, familiar with these surroundings from the images gathered when she connected with his soul in the hospital.

A shudder flooded her system as her eyes spotted the window. They were similar to those in Melissa's house and brought back memories of when the Guardians had called to her from the grassed area below with news of Toren's vampirism. Rochelle struggled to focus on the mission. She tried to turn her attention to another area of the room, but her eyes refused to stray from the windows. Without conscious thought, she moved forward and touched the glass. Cameron glided to the spot beside her. "Are you okay?"

"No," she said, turning tear-filled eyes in his direction.

"What is the matter?" he asked, reaching for her. He had forgotten, once again, that he was unable to make physical contact. "Sorry," he mumbled.

"It's fine," she sniffled, pressing her forehead against the glass. She pulled a ring out of her pocket and showed it to him. A white gold band housed a perfect solitaire diamond. "My boyfriend had been saving this for our anniversary. He was finally going to propose. He had it with him when they found his body."

"What happened to him?"

"He was bitten by a wild animal. He developed an infection the doctors couldn't cure."

"I am so sorry, Rochelle."

"It isn't your fault he died." She blew her nose with a tissue before continuing, "But it will be my fault if you do."

"No, you are wrong. Responsibility for my death will lie with the people who have done this to me. Promise me something?"

"What?" she threw the tissue in a bin.

"You will avenge my death if you can't save me."

Rochelle's gaze never flinched, "These people are dangerous, Cameron. We cannot allow them the freedom to do this or worse to others. Either way, they will be found and dealt with. You have my word."

Cameron grinned sadly. "Where shall we start?"

"I'm not sure," she admitted. "I can't feel the presence of adverse energy in the room."

"Do you think Mum might have put the necklace in her room?"

"It's possible. She would want to feel close to you at all times."

"You don't think she is wearing it, do you?" he said fearfully.

"I don't know," Rochelle said, walking towards the door. "Where is her room?"

"You can't go in there," he squealed.

"You don't have to come. We don't have time to wait until morning. The sooner we get you back into your body, the better."

"You'll find them at the other end of the hall," he flicked his head in their direction.

"I'll be back in a minute."

Rochelle was gone for quite some time. Cameron was pacing the floor when she returned. She watched him silently, her lips twitching with amusement. He spotted her a few seconds after her arrival and scowled at her crossly. "What took you so long? You said you would be back in a minute!"

"Look at you keeping track of time."

His energy shimmered with displeasure. "Did you find it?"

"No," she confessed. "I nearly got caught when my phone dinged with a message. Chandra found a hex bag in your hospital room. It was complicated magic that was very powerful. Although she has separated the contents of the sachet, the magic contained in each component is still active. Her plan is to keep it far away from you until the containment box we have ordered arrives. It is up to us to locate the necklace and get it to her before the reaper comes for you."

"Easier said than done," Cameron moaned. "Do you believe it could be somewhere else in the house?"

"It is possible. Chandra mentioned that the hex bag was cloaked. She would have had no way of sensing its presence if the nurse had not dislodged it from its position."

"So, what do we do now? Search the house from top to bottom or head on over to Melissa's place."

"I have a better idea," Rochelle smirked.

"Are you going to tell me or keep it to yourself?" he asked impatiently.

"Any chance your mother talks in her sleep?"

"Are you crazy?" his energy swirled with intense emotion.

"Yep," she answered, walking out of the room.

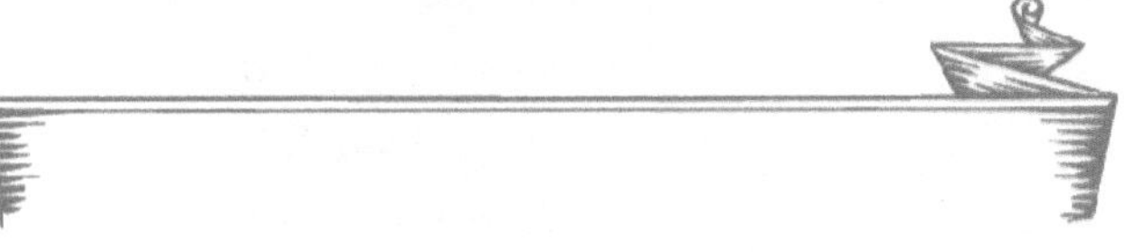
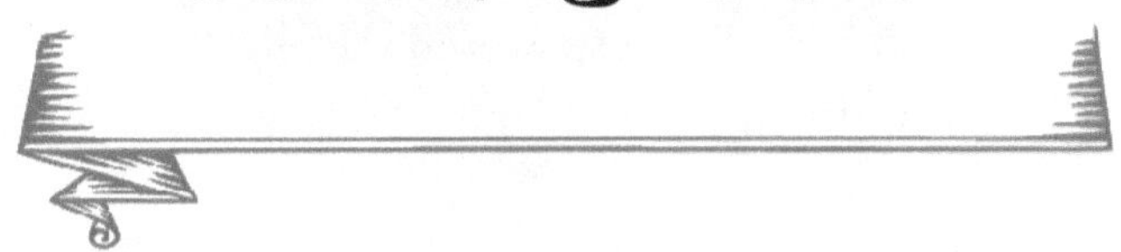

Twenty-Two

Rochelle would have liked nothing better than to link with Karen's mind and search for the information she required. The human brain was fragile. She had already connected with her previously and didn't want to run the risk of causing permanent damage. That possibility was only considered acceptable when a human became aware of the Gatherer's extraordinary abilities or the existence of the Locator Fairies at which time the memories containing that evidence would be wiped.

To get the information she needed, Rochelle would have to become creative. She snuck back into their room and paused as Johnathon rolled over. He draped his arm over Karen's shoulder, causing her to shift slightly in her sleep. Rochelle counted to five before moving further into the room. She changed her appearance, aging her outward traits to those of a fit eighty year old. Her battlesuit morphed into a seafoam turtleneck sweater and dusty rose trousers. Her feet were encased in white coloured sneakers and her white hair was rolled into a French bun.

Rochelle perched herself on the side of the bed and whispered, "Karen, I've got a crucial question for you."

"Hmmm, okay," she answered sleepily.

"What did you do with the necklace David willed to Cameron?"

"The solicitor gave it to Cameron," she murmured.

"What happened to the necklace after Cameron's accident?"

"The nurses took it off him."

"Did they give it to you?"

"No, they gave it to Johnathon."

Rochelle jolted when Johnathon's voice joined in on the conversation. "You are sleep-talking again, Karen."

"What?" she grumbled, lifting her head and opening her eyes. "Who the hell are you?"

"Your mystical angel, Karen. I am the one who gives you your visions."

"You are?" her eyes widened and her voice rose an octave.

Johnathon sat up in bed, blinking the sleep from his eyes. "Get the hell out of our room."

Rochelle changed herself back into a fly. In the blink of an eye, she had disappeared from their view. Karen said, "Did you see that?"

"Yes, but I don't believe it. Go back to sleep, Karen. We must be dreaming."

"The same dream?" she questioned.

"Being married as long as we have, I guess we were bound to begin thinking alike."

"That's ridiculous," Karen stated firmly. "Come back, Angel. Ask your questions, and we will answer."

"Now who's being ridiculous," Johnathon raged. "An angel wouldn't need to ask you questions. They already know everything."

"Not everything," Rochelle said, returning to human form. "I need to know what happened to David's necklace."

"Why?" Johnathon asked, barely able to get the word out.

"It has been cursed," she admitted truthfully.

"Cursed?" Karen's hand flew up to Johnathon's chest. "Where is it, John?"

"I gave it to Candice for safe-keeping. She is the right girl for our Cameron, and you did say they would get married someday."

Karen gave Johnathon the sweetest smile. "You felt a connection with her?'

He nodded his head, "It was the strangest thing."

"We'll have to get it off her tomorrow when she comes to visit him. She can't be walking around with a cursed item hanging around her neck."

Rochelle tapped the pair on their shoulders and said, "You leave that to me. Go back to sleep, and may God be with you."

She then repeated her disappearing act and flew back to Cameron.

"Well," he said, the moment he spotted her.

"Candice has it," she informed him.

"Does that mean she is in danger now?" he asked.

"Yes," Rochelle stated quietly. "Do you know where she is?"

He disappeared. Rochelle threw her hands in the air, "Great!" She flopped on the bed and waited for his return. The sun came up and he still wasn't home, leaving her too much time to think.

She was a blubbering mess from being on her own with her memories of Toren and dwelling on all she had lost, when she heard movement down the hall. Rochelle bounded to her feet and stepped behind the door in case his parents entered the room. When she heard the stairs creaking beneath two sets of feet, she knew she was safe. She waited patiently while they prepared themselves for the day and as soon as they left the house, grabbed some tissues and cleaned her face, then made her way back to the hospital.

The reaper was there to greet her, though she couldn't see him. He was disappointed to see her alone. He had hoped the sisters were capable of keeping a leash on the boy for longer than a few hours. It seemed he was wrong, again. He followed her upstairs and entered the room behind her. He was interested in watching her apply her latest plan of action.

She smiled at the nurse and walked to the top of the bed. "Hello, Cameron. Remember me? We are going to get that blood circulating in your body in preparation for your return. Don't keep us waiting too much longer, hey."

Wang narrowed his eyes, wondering if there was an underlying message in there. He glanced at his list to see that Cameron's name was almost the same depth of colour as the others. *Nearly out of time, Gatherer.* The reaper observed the placement of her hands on his body and waited curiously. He felt the energy exuded by her fingertips and developed a suspicion of what she hoped to accomplish.

She could not heal his body completely. The interest that would stir in the medical world would not be conducive to her kind remaining under the radar of the humans. A little bit of energy directed to the right place could be enough to call his soul back to his body. Although he didn't breathe, Wang's chest tightened as he paused expectantly. Within a few minutes, Cameron's spirit arrived. A grin spread across Rochelle's face as Wang's eyebrow rose with admiration.

Cameron baulked when he eyed the reaper. "I think we are too late," he said to Rochelle, pointing a finger in Wang's direction.

"No, we are not," she denied. "Chandra destroyed the hex bag, and you are no longer in possession of the necklace."

"The reaper is here," Cameron advised her.

Rochelle looked at the empty space where Cameron indicated. "You can't have him! We did what you asked, we've removed the obstacles in his path."

The nurse looked at her full of concern, "You all right, Rochelle? Who are you talking to, love?"

"Nobody," she said sheepishly. "Sorry. I am writing a book and wanted to hear what the words would sound like if said verbally."

"Well, it sounds like you are warning somebody off," she stated helpfully. "Is that what you were hoping for?"

"Sure is," she laughed, manoeuvring Cameron's wrist gently in her hands.

"What is the story going to be about?" the nurse inquired.

She gazed at Cameron fearfully. When she noticed his calm demeanour, she relaxed a little. "Actually, the story is inspired by Cameron here," Rochelle stated, choosing not to elaborate further.

"Really, in what way?"

Rochelle lowered her eyes, not wanting the woman to see her reaction. She really wished she could tamper with the nurse's mind, but she had done that already. "It is going to be about a guy who has an accident so traumatic, his soul has ripped away from his body. His spirit is going to be given a set of challenges to complete before he can become whole once more. In the meantime, he has caught the attention of a reaper intent on capturing his soul. The story, I hope, will be a thrilling race to see who crosses the finish line first."

"Wow," she said. "That sounds awesome. I'd love to read that when you're finished."

"Me, too," Rochelle grinned.

"How is it going to end? NO! Don't tell me," she said louder than usual. "You'll spoil the ending."

Rochelle took a deep breath. She didn't know how the story was going to end, yet. She peeked at the nurse through her peripheral vision, then mouthed to Cameron, "Are you safe?"

He nodded his head, "For now."

Rochelle moved further up his arm, manipulating his muscles confidently, "Where is Candice?" she murmured quietly, hoping he would hear her.

"On her way here," he confirmed.

"I think you should amalgamate," she ran her hands over his body so there was no confusion to the meaning of her statement. Cameron would have refused if the reaper had not concurred with her announcement. Cameron needed to know Candice was safe. He planned on reuniting with her to make sure she got to the hospital safely.

The fact that the reaper was back in his room gave him cause for concern. If he were to reap Cameron's soul, there would be no way of protecting her anyway, and his death would put all of humanity in danger. With a touch of nervousness, he floated towards the bed, aligning his body up for a perfect fit.

"Keep my loved ones safe," he pleaded.

"Always," Rochelle whispered.

He lowered himself slowly, tensing slightly against the barrier he expected to meet. Instead, he settled into his body like it was a well-worn sleeping bag. His body became defensive temporarily as the soul began its invasion.

After a few seconds, flesh and blood recognised the composition of returning energy and welcomed its presence gratefully. It was not long after that, his throat attempted to expel the tube that had been helping him breathe. His gag-reflex kicked in, surprising the nurse and Rochelle into action. The woman shouted orders at Rochelle, who followed them unfalteringly. Approval shone in the nurse's eyes as she continued to make Cameron more comfortable.

He tried to open his eyes but found he was too tired to achieve even that feat. The fact that he could no longer communicate with Rochelle frustrated him to no end. He lay on the bed with eyes that refused to open and a body that declined to follow his commands, and yet he was incredibly grateful to be alive and safe from the reaper's clutches. He knew it wouldn't be long before he would be capable of sitting up to talk to his family and friends. For now, he would take whatever time he could get to rest because once his mother found out he was awake, sleep-time would be over.

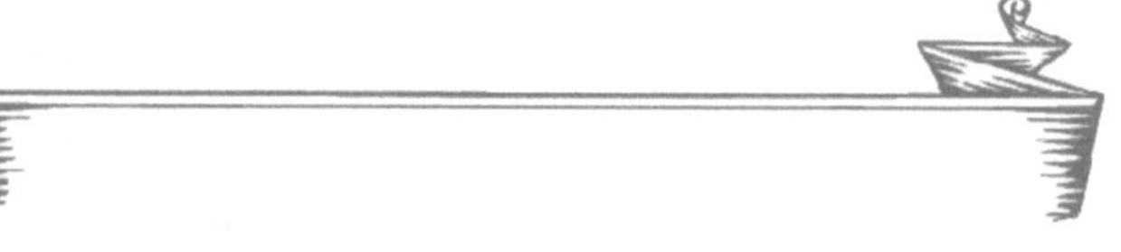

Twenty-Three

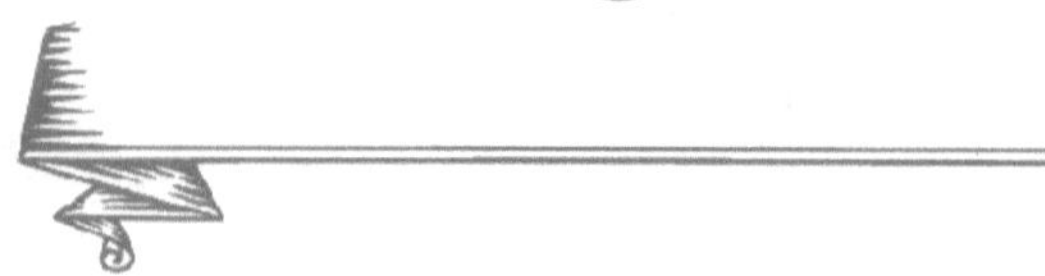

Rochelle continued ministering to Cameron's muscles which had atrophied slightly during his stay. She viewed his rising chest with a modicum of pride and couldn't wait for his family to arrive to observe him breathing on his own. Rochelle chatted happily as she worked, hoping the soothing tone of her voice would keep him relaxed while his body readjusted.

It was half an hour before he received his first visitor of the day. Karen walked in with the air of someone prepared to settle in for the majority of the day to hold a one-way conversation. Imagine her surprise when she discovered the tubes had been removed from his throat, and the heart monitor was beeping at a faster pace than she was used to. The room was quieter without the hiss of the ventilator. Karen's hand flew to her mouth as she choked out her question, "Is he awake?"

"No," the duty nurse answered cheerfully. "Though, his condition has improved, and he is breathing on his own."

"Why didn't you call us?" Karen scowled.

"You were already on your way. There was no point in risking an accident of your own."

"But Johnathon isn't with me this morning. He had a meeting to attend to."

"Why don't you leave him a message to contact you as soon as possible? Be sure to tell him nothing is wrong. Cameron is out of the coma but will take a few hours to wake up, yet. He has been through a lot, and you will need to be patient with him. Don't try to hurry the process. Just keep talking to him as you would any other day. He will begin to interact when he is ready, though his throat will be sore and his voice will be rather raspy."

"We can work with that," Karen smiled broadly. "Were you here when he woke, Rochelle?"

"I sure was. The two of us unplugged him from the machines. It was a fantastic experience though I'm glad you weren't there to see it."

Karen gauged the underlying meaning and agreed. She'd watched many medical shows on television and could just imagine the distress he must have gone through coming out of unconsciousness. "I'll just pop outside and call my husband."

"We'll still be here when you return," Rochelle assured her.

"You will be, my shift was over fifteen minutes ago."

"Where's your replacement?"

"Right here," Chandra said, sweeping into the room. Her hair was auburn instead of blonde, and her eyes had changed from brown to hazel. She had grown twenty centimetres taller, but her voice remained the same as did her natural stride as she sauntered towards the bed.

Rochelle looked puzzled as she linked their minds. *What are you doing here?*

Chandra pretended to listen to the nurse as she discussed the changes in his condition. She nodded occasionally and made simple noises, hoping they were of the correct tone and inserted in the appropriate places.

"So you are returning to the living, young man," Chandra said, leaning over to peer into his face, once the nurse had finished her spiel. "All going well, we will be moving him to a ward after lunch. Will you continue to tend to his needs after he is relocated?" she asked Rochelle.

"Possibly." Rochelle waved to the nurse, "Loved working with you. You were awesome."

The nurse smiled back, "Can't wait to read the book."

Rochelle giggled merrily, the nurse tickling her funny bone.

"What was that all about?" Chandra asked as the woman exited through the door.

"I'll tell you later."

"So, our Jack is back in the box."

"Yes," Rochelle agreed.

"Not surprising really, considering we found the hex bag and excised it from his room. Samuel personally delivered the containment box this morning. Do you know him?"

"Yes, I know the stuffy muffin."

Chandra burst into laughter, "Yeah that about sums him up. God, what a stick in the mud."

"Yes, he is. Very knowledgeable on a countless number of creatures, but hasn't got a clue on how to interact with humankind."

"Pity, he is quite a looker," Chandra fanned her face with her hand.

"Really?" Rochelle spluttered, never having set eyes on him herself.

"What's the story with the necklace? I've hidden the containment box in the carpark with a triangular formation of crystals for protection."

"You had some on your person when the guardians abducted you?"

"Kidnapped, you mean," she scowled.

"Semantics," Rochelle shrugged. "Candice has it. She is on her way in."

"Estimated time of arrival?"

"Unknown," Rochelle confirmed. "Do you have any idea what you are doing?"

"Sure," Chandra smirked. "I have spent hundreds of years in the medical field in the States. There is nothing I don't know how to do."

"Using human technology or the enhancements we gained by becoming a Gatherer?"

"Both," she chuckled softly.

Karen walked in with Candice in tow. "Rochelle, you haven't met Candice. She is Cameron's fiancé."

"Really?" she smiled at the girl. "He's a bit young to be thinking about getting married, isn't he?"

"They are going to have a long engagement, aren't you, sweetheart? You can tell they are soul mates just by looking at the two of them together."

"That's a nice ring you have there," Chandra said, admiring the golden band with an emerald stone. "The necklace is interesting."

"It belongs to Cameron. I'm just taking care of it for him while he is in here."

"Did Karen tell you he is improving?"

"Yes," her smile reached her eyes.

"You can put it in the drawer there," Chandra pointed to a cupboard beside the heart monitor, "if you like. Once Cameron is capable of sitting up, we can put it back on him."

"That's okay," she said more confidently than she felt, "I'd like to give it to him myself."

"Suit yourself."

Rochelle said her goodbyes and left the room. Having completed her therapy from top to bottom, she had run out of excuses to stay. She knew that Chandra would keep a close eye on him in her absence. She wondered how Chandra had managed to wrangle the real nurse away from her post. Probably best if she didn't ask questions she didn't want the answers to.

With Cameron's soul safe and the necklace out of her reach, she wondered what to do with her time. She wasn't ready to be by herself again, after this morning. Too much pain awaited her that she wasn't prepared to face on her own. Johnathon was at work, and as Keeley wasn't present, Melissa must be home watching over her. That left only one thing for her to do. She would start hunting the witches that had manipulated Cameron's lifeline.

It was a weird feeling second-guessing herself. Before Toren was bitten and Chandra had returned, Rochelle would have been all over the mission.

Instead, she had found herself unsure of what steps to take that would end in Cameron's safety. Not to mention the fear that arose whenever she thought of hunting the witches herself. She wasn't sure when she had started to feel afraid.

Rochelle was not accustomed to weakness, and she didn't like it. The only way she was going to get past her emotional panic was to face it, head-on. "Bring it!" she shouted to the universe. Rochelle ran to her car and navigated the streets with the expertise of a local. She pulled into the same spot she'd parked in earlier and jogged through the park until she reached the trunk of Tianna's tree.

"Yo, T. You in there?" she called softly.

Tianna yanked open the door and rushed towards her with an anxious face. "Were you able to save Cameron?"

"His soul has returned to his body, though he is still asleep."

"So the universes are safe, and we can go back to protecting the humans."

"Not quite, T. The witches are out there, and we are the only ones who can stop them from attempting this again."

"How do you propose to do that? They haven't even pinged our radar."

"Why would they?" Rochelle leant her shoulder against the bark. "They are indigenous to the planet.

Your skills are better suited to locating and identifying non-indigenous species."

"So, how do you expect me to help you with the witches?"

"You were able to see Cameron's soul. Why not magic-wielding humans?"

Tianna landed on a limb nearest to Rochelle's face. She lowered herself gingerly until she was in a seated position. Her palms rested on the top of the branch for balance while her legs swung freely beneath her. She sent out a pulse of energy that radiated three hundred and sixty degrees, searching for feelings of malicious intent with a twist of devilish fervour. Once the pulse reached the boundary of her sector, it fizzled out as she intended. "There is a furious woman in the vicinity of your cabin that might be worth checking out. Her hatred for people is astonishing."

Rochelle frowned, "How close to my cottage?"

"Pretty close," Tianna confirmed.

"Feel up for a drive?"

"In the Ferrari?"

"Yes," Rochelle laughed.

"Pull my door closed, will ya?" Tianna yelled, already flying towards the car.

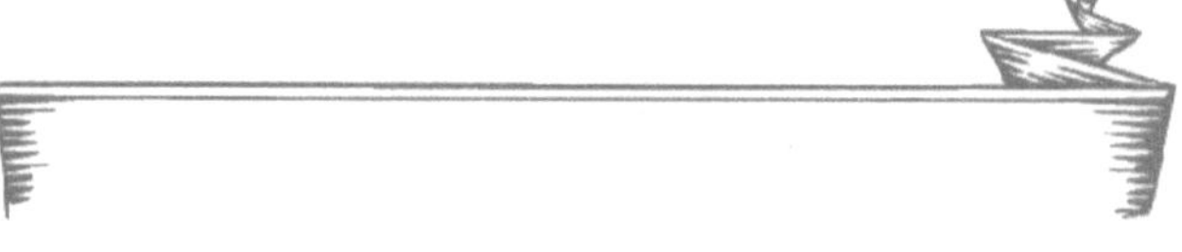

Twenty-Four

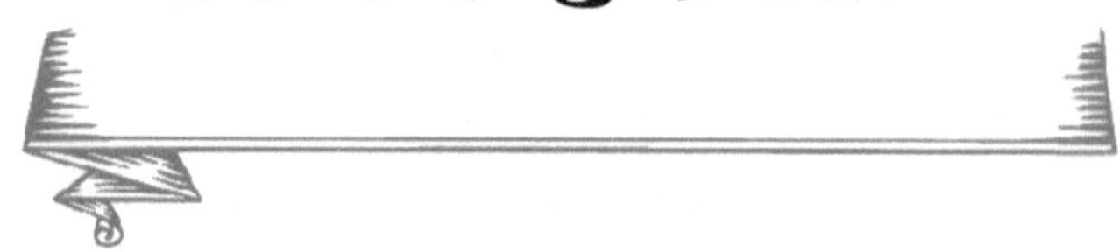

Rochelle was not that surprised when Tianna led her directly to the cabin. She'd had an inkling that Chandra had done something when she had arrived at the hospital with a changed appearance. Her gut had warned her that something was afoot. When Tianna had pinpointed the location to a spot near her cabin, Rochelle had wondered if the nurse was being held inside for interrogation at a later date. What she hadn't concluded was the reason why.

Still, to enter the front door and be confronted with the image in front of her was disturbing, to say the least. The woman was tied to a kitchen chair with zip ties and blindfolded with a black brassiere from Rochelle's drawer. *'Never going to wear that again,'* she thought. The hair on her arms and the nape of her neck were standing on their ends. The pieces of the puzzle finally fell into place. The witches had foreseen this woman's current circumstance. They used the image of this concept as inspiration for the vision they had sent Karen.

The witches were onto them and had been from the beginning. Were they aware that Cameron was not going to be the catalyst to their doomsday plans? Rochelle didn't know, but it was definitely time to find out. She stepped further into the room. The woman raised her head further as she heard Rochelle's approach. "Who's there?" her frightened voice quivered.

"My name is Rochelle. Why did my sister bring you here?"

"I don't know," she said. "Your sister is crazy. Untie me, please."

"I don't think so," Rochelle grabbed a chair and placed it in front of the woman's. She swung a leg over the seat and relaxed her arms on the backrest as she plonked herself on the plush, cushioned surface, "You are a nurse?"

"Yes," the woman frowned, which was lost beneath the cups of the bra.

"Who were you reporting to?"

"The head nurse," she returned, confusion lacing her voice.

"The witches, where will I find them?"

"Witches," the woman laughed. "You are as crazy as your sister."

Rochelle felt she was wasting her time. She tapped into the woman's mind and searched for the information she needed. She found nothing of value except that the nurse was given a phone number to text when Cameron's body expired but had no idea where her contact was located or any details about them that could lead to a current location.

Hidden deeply in her mind was the information that the nurse was the one who had placed the hex bag under the mattress of Cameron's bed. There was no information to be gathered of who had given it to her in the first place. Rochelle rang the Starlight Investigation team and was delighted to be connected with Sophia.

She updated her on the situation and asked her to trace the owner of the phone number. It turned out to be a burner phone but had the GPS locator turned off. When she tried to turn it on remotely, Sophia found her attempt unsuccessful. They concluded the phone was under a protection spell and that their lead had ended up being a dead end.

Rochelle asked Sophia to keep her apprised of any energy spikes detected by the Starlight team. She hoped that the level of magic the witches were conjuring would show up on their sensor equipment similar to that of higher than average electricity usage. Sophia promised to have an agent collect the woman within the hour.

Rochelle slumped on the chair. "What now, Tianna?"

"I suppose we wait," she stated forlornly. *"It's disheartening to know there is a major threat out there that we can't detect with our senses."*

"Can't your magic recognise the magic in others?"

"Yes, but we have to be close enough to detect its existence and usage. The areas we cover are quite large for a creature so little. The fact that they are using power accessible to all makes it that much more difficult."

"I wonder how Chandra found the witches in the States?"

"You'll have to ask her when you see her. I am guessing they were found during a regular human investigation. Humans are quite capable of finding their own monsters, Rochelle."

"Yes, you are right. That must have been how she became aware of them. That doesn't help us, though."

"Sometimes it takes the humans years to hunt down a criminal. We'll have to be patient and sabotage the witches' plans wherever we can until we can learn their identities and lock them up for good."

"In the meantime?"

"I'll send out a warning to my kin. Ask them to keep a lookout for unnatural behaviours and energies in the human world."

"What should I do?" Rochelle asked, terrified of spending time on her own. "Chandra will be tied up at the hospital for the remainder of this woman's shift. If I can't determine the location of the witches . . ."

"Why don't you go home and jump on the internet? Surely there are some searches you could do to narrow down the location we should be concentrating on. The witches can't be too far away. You could look for news articles that report strange occurrences in the area."

"That's a great idea," Rochelle stated. "I'll do that as soon as she is collected. Want to hang around with me for a little while? I could drop you at home afterwards."

"That would be great," she gave an embarrassed grin. *"I seem to have forgotten to bring my homing device in my excitement of having another ride in the Ferrari."*

Rochelle wandered into the kitchen. "I don't have any flowers or mushrooms in my cupboards, but I do have a peach in my cooler. Would that be okay for you to eat?"

"Sure, I love peaches," Tianna fluttered to the countertop. She watched Rochelle prepare the table for brunch and took note of the sadness underlying her movements. She knew that Rochelle would be

okay in time, but wished she could do something to help her now. Rochelle sliced a small piece of peach for Tianna, placing it in the lid of a 500mL juice bottle.

She grimaced at the lack of cutlery suitably sized for a fairy and set a wet-wipe on the counter for her to use to clean her hands. Rochelle drank the juice and ate a couple of pieces of cheese on toast. They chatted amicably while they waited for the agent to arrive.

Chandra kept a watchful eye on Cameron's vitals while his mum and girlfriend sat with him. His mum talked about the conversations she had been having with the Principal of his school and Candice spoke about the places they could go to on future dates. Cameron took it all in, though he couldn't indicate he had heard their words.

He was inwardly pleased to learn he would be graduating with honours even though he would miss his final exams. His teachers had agreed to use his grades for term three as his final result and the Education Department had approved this decision.

He would lose the opportunity to attend his senior formal, which he discovered he was not that upset over. Two of his friends were dead, and he had no idea how the twins were doing in their own fight for survival. Candice was not a student and would be ineligible to attend the event.

He was excited to discover Candice had been thinking about ways they could spend more time together. He looked forward to being able to talk to her when his body was ready to respond. He hoped that his injuries would not scar too severely and she would not be turned off by anything she might see.

He gave himself a mental slap. Candice was not the kind of girl who viewed people through superficial eyes. She had proven that already. She would accept him; however he came out of this. Besides, his mum had seen their wedding day.

He listened to them talking in turns as though Candice had been part of the family for ages. His heart swelled with joy that her assimilation into their family was as seamless and welcoming as David's had been. He hoped their lives together would last a lot longer than what was offered to Melissa. Even if it wasn't, he promised to love Candice every day of his life as though it was their last. If nothing else, his experiences had taught him life could be short, and you had to take whatever you could with both hands.

His mind went to sleep; the energy levels required to concentrate intently on what was being said was exhausting. When he woke, he was in the company of Keeley and his dad. He could hear his dad talking to him about a unicorn, and realised he was telling him a story that Keeley had made up for him.

The unicorn carried Princess Keeley into the forest where she was met by the fairy queen, who grew to be the same size as the young girl. The fairy queen gazed at her with admiration for the courage she displayed in travelling such a long distance to fight for the right to win the potion that would wake her uncle from his sleep. Princess Keeley glared at the queen with challenging eyes. "I need that potion," she said with a steely voice. "I will do whatever it takes to get it."

The queen raised an eyebrow. "Is that so?" she asked. Princess Keeley nodded her head with a determined frown.

"I like your resolve, little one, and would like to offer you the most wonderful gift I possess."

"What is it?" The princess asked excitedly, momentarily forgetting her place.

The queen hid a smile behind her hand, "The gift I have for you is not something you can carry with you in your pocket. Nor is it something you should easily pass onto someone else. The gift I have for you is for you alone, young one."

The princess wriggled slightly in her saddle. "Tell me," she demanded a little crossly, desperate to return to her uncle with the cure.

"The potion you seek has been with you the whole time."

"What is it?" she said, leaning forward expectantly.

"A few shavings from the horn of your unicorn sprinkled over his body will wake him up safe and well."

"Are you telling the truth?" the princess asked, having heard that fairies could be tricky beings.

The queen raised her left arm diagonally across her chest, "Fairy's honour."

Princess Keeley dismounted her unicorn to hug the fairy queen. "Thank you so much," she said gratefully. The fairy queen was taken by surprise but quickly snuggled into the embrace, enjoying the sensation enormously.

"Hurry along, little one," she encouraged. "Time is ticking away."

Princess Keeley launched herself at the unicorn and rode like the wind to her castle's infirmary. She hurried up the stairs and knelt on the chair beside her uncle's bed. She removed the lid of a tiny glass container that held a few sprinkles of the unicorn's horn. She tipped the contents onto her hand and then spread them over his sleeping body. "Awaken, Pwince Camwon," Keeley cried theatrically.

Cameron's eye twitched as a few scatterings of glitter hit the skin below. He heard Keeley's gasp, "Did you see that, Grandad?"

"See what, Poppet?"

"His eye winked in his sleep."

"Did it?" at her affirmative nod, he continued, "Perhaps the unicorn dust is working?"

"Do you weally think so?" she asked, her voice filled with hope.

"Ah, Keeley, I think you might have found the answer to Cameron's sleepiness."

She was quiet for a little bit. Cameron could imagine her giving her grandfather a huge hug. He put everything he had into saying her name. All he could manage was the letter, K.

Johnathon sprung to his feet and shifted Keeley onto his hip. Chandra rushed forward and shone a light into his eyes. "It's all good, Cameron," she said gently. "Take your time." She raised her eyes to see tears shining in Johnathon's. She leant forward and squeezed his hand, then rubbed a hand up Keeley's arm. "Well done, you. I knew I was making the right decision when your Grandad asked if I could sneak you in so he could tell Cameron the story you wrote for him. There is no way it would have worked as well if you weren't in the room, Keeley. It must stay our secret though."

Keeley nodded her head while opening her mouth wide as she took a humungous breath. "I knew the unicorn could save him. It helped the King and Queen's people's teeth get better when they ate lollies all the time."

"You did great, kiddo," Chandra said. "He will be talking to you in no time."

"What do you mean? He talks to me all the time."

Johnathon stared at his granddaughter. "You could see Cameron at our house, couldn't you, dear?"

"Yes," she replied unabashedly.

"Why did you say you couldn't?"

"Camwon told me to."

Johnathon nodded his head, "You should listen to your elders."

"That's what mummy says," she agreed.

"Is Cameron the only invisible person you've seen?"

Keeley shrugged her shoulders, "It's a bit hard to tell."

"Hmmm," Johnathon replied. "Is he waking?" he asked Chandra.

"He has been conscious on and off for a little while. He is weak. It will be some time before he will be able to open his eyes for any length of time. Talking will take longer. Be patient with him."

"Of course," he said, grabbing Cameron's hand in his own. "He can have as much time as he needs. I should go and get his mother."

"That's not necessary. Stay a while longer but Keeley will need to go outside before another staff member catches her in here."

"Keeley can come with me. His mother and sister should spend some time with him."

Chandra went back to monitoring the machines. Karen and Melissa walked into the room and took up their respective chairs. Melissa leant forward and placed the necklace around Cameron's neck. "Candice is waiting outside for you to wake, Cameron. She wanted to give this to you herself, but hopes having it returned to you will give you the incentive to wake up faster."

Chandra was dismayed to see it around Cameron's neck once more. She knew the danger the object possessed especially to somebody who had already been affected by its wickedness. She wondered how she was going to eliminate the endangerment without them realising the item had gone missing.

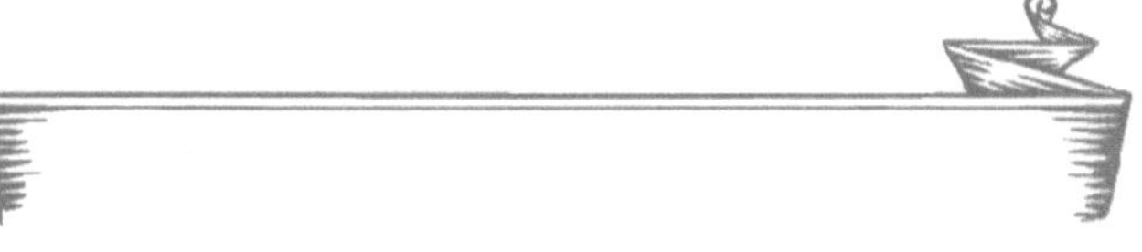

Twenty-Five

True to her word, Rochelle took Tianna home as soon as the woman was taken away. She did not, however, return to her house to research the internet. That would have been impossible considering her place of residence was in another state. She did not want to board at Toren's house either. Too many memories awaited her inside the walls.

Instead, she chose to utilise the services of the local library, which meant becoming a member. Easier said than done with an interstate drivers licence. Her application firmly denied, she wandered around without direction or purpose. With no other way to pursue the witches and not having taken the time to make friends with anyone other than Toren, Force and April, who were all unavailable, the only place left for her to go was back to the hospital. She just had to come up with an applicable explanation for being there.

Once she walked into the ward, she discovered she had no reason to be concerned. Johnathon welcomed her like an old friend, updating her on Cameron's progress. Rochelle didn't have the heart to tell him she already knew he was on his way back. She allowed him the luxury of explaining things to a person who had shown a keen interest in his progress.

Rochelle loved every minute of their interaction. She marvelled over Keeley's bright idea of unicorn dust to rouse him from sleep. The way Keeley proudly puffed out her chest brought a tear to Rochelle's eyes. Johnathon encouraged her to pop into Cameron's room even though she had performed her duties already that morning. Rochelle realised she had begun to develop feelings for the family. She cared about their wellbeing and decided she would keep tabs on them long after Cameron had made a full recovery.

Feelings of dread rolled through the room in waves. Rochelle frowned with unease as she glanced at each occupant, her focus then becoming centred on her sister. She glared at her as mind-link was established. *"What is going on?"*

"The necklace is back on Cameron. I don't know how to remove it without causing suspicion."

"Leave it to me." Rochelle strolled over to the bed. "His colour is looking great."

"Your physio sessions have done a world of good, Rochelle," Karen said.

"You are too kind," she flashed her a smile. "I think we should take this off until he has recovered more fully." Rochelle reached for the chain.

"Candice wanted him to have it back," Melissa scowled slightly. "She thought it would help him recover faster."

"I've no doubt about that," Rochelle nodded. "However, he has been unconscious for quite a while. His injuries were severe. The last thing he needs is an item that might cause infection. Why don't I take it downstairs for cleaning?"

Karen appeared relieved, "That would be wonderful," she agreed.

Rochelle gazed at her firmly. "He might not get it back today."

"That's fine," she waved her hand in the air. "He can have it back when it is safe," she said.

Rochelle opened the clasp and removed the necklace from his neck. She placed it in her pocket, being careful to keep the medallion intact. She sent a wink in her sister's direction. "I'm glad he is doing better."

Karen nodded, and Melissa smiled.

"How are your studies going, Melissa?"

"Really well, considering."

"Have you been granted any extensions?"

"With Mum and Dad's help, I don't think I'll need them."

"That's great news. See you tomorrow?"

"See you tomorrow," they replied in unison.

Rochelle went to the carpark quickly and searched for the crystals. She spotted them easily. They were a bunch of rocks originating from the planet Mystique that emitted an energy signature not found on our planet. She used one of her elemental powers to breach the surface of the dome and retrieved the box. She opened it cautiously, being careful not to spill its contents, then placed the necklace and medallion carefully on the cushioned surface. She replaced the lid and retrieved the crystals, placing them in her pocket. Rochelle jumped in the car and called Starlight Investigations.

She put the coordinates of the nearest agent into her navigation system and spun the wheels as she took off. She pushed the play button on the stereo, and the speakers started blaring the soundtrack to the Sound of Music. Rochelle howled with laughter as tears sprang from her eyes. "I'm going to miss you, honey," she cried. Rochelle sang along to every song, not the least bit concerned by the stares received from other road users.

She handed the box over with a great deal of relief. Once the business of securing the objects was out of the way, she took the time to enjoy the attraction of the man standing before her. He was tall with broad shoulders, thin waist and tight butt. Short brown hair that was slicked back at the sides and slightly longer in the back moulded an almond-shaped face with a strong chin, small stubby nose, and deep chocolate eyes. He was not in the same league as Toren, but he was not that far below the rung that he wouldn't have turned her eye at a happier time in her life. It wasn't until he spoke that she realised who he was.

"We'll take great care with this, Rochelle. You can be sure it will never see the light of day again."

She was so surprised she stammered her response. "Th..thanks, Samuel. There is a necklace in there that I need to be cleansed or copied. What are my chances?"

"We don't have anyone available to do a cleansing at this point in time. How detailed is the necklace? Are there any expensive stones involved?"

"No stones, but there is a medallion with an angel embossing."

"Hmmm, that could take a couple of days to arrange the services of one of our jewellers. I'll take a look at it when I get it back to the office and can place it in a decontamination cabinet."

"Will that take away the curse?"

"No, but it will stop any surface contaminants from leaving the objects and attaching themselves to me."

"What about us?" Rochelle asked aghast.

"You will be fine. You are Gatherers."

"What has that got to do with anything?"

"Everything," he blinked.

"What about Cameron?"

"Your phantasm?" Rochelle nodded her head. "He will be immune to its immediate effects. If he was to continue wearing it, it would continue to cause havoc in his life."

"What about his girlfriend? She has been wearing it for a few days."

"That complicates matters. Text through her details, and we will take care of it."

"Right," Rochelle replied. "Anything else?"

"Not at the moment. You did a great job of saving the boy, Rochelle, considering everything you are going through. We want you to know how sorry we are for your loss and to let you know you are not alone."

Tears welled up in her eyes for the umpteenth time. "Thanks, Samuel. I appreciate your thoughts. See you around?"

He refrained from answering, simply stared at her until she felt uncomfortable enough to return to her car. The return journey took longer with more traffic on the road. She replayed the soundtrack and sang at the top of her lungs. She was a few minutes late when she pulled up at the hospital.

Chandra sat quietly on a chair, listening to an elderly lady cursing her family for their lack of compassion. Chandra was accommodating and polite even after she'd spotted the car. She waited until an appropriate gap in the conversation to inform the lady that her ride had arrived. The woman patted her on the hand and thanked her for listening. Chandra wished her a good day and jumped in the car. She waited until Rochelle had pulled away from the curb before asking what she had been up to.

Rochelle let her know the package had been delivered and she hoped to have a replacement necklace in a few days. Chandra showed her surprise at Rochelle's thoughtfulness, making Rochelle blush. She drove them to the nearest burger shop and ordered a considerable feed. She figured Chandra had earned the right to put her feet up and enjoy a quiet night at home. Not knowing what her favourite food was, she thought a fast food shop would have something on the menu to excite her tastebuds.

Rochelle soon discovered that even though some of our supply chains had the same names as those in the States, the taste of the food was quite different from what Chandra was used to. She was quick to point out that the food was not distasteful, it was simply different. After she had finished her meal, Rochelle asked after Cameron.

"He will probably be up and talking tomorrow for short bursts. They will most likely move him in the morning. I managed to keep him where he was today. I made sure the afternoon team would leave him where he was, and they won't risk moving him during the night shift. Hopefully, the witches don't have anyone else on staff."

"Do you think they will try again?"

"I don't know. Maybe we should stay with him, at least until he is released from the hospital."

"Do you usually suffer from separation anxiety?" Rochelle queried lightly.

Chandra appeared offended, "You're not afraid to walk away?"

Rochelle grimaced at being called out. "Sure, I am, but we can't hover over our humans, Chandra. We have to give them the chance to live their lives as they were meant to."

"We need to make sure they are safe before walking away."

"Touché."

The girls hopped in the car and headed back to the hospital. "You are going to pay for this portion of parking fees, Chandra."

"Fine," she shrugged. "I'll take it out of next week's pay."

"Doing what?" Rochelle raised her eyebrows.

"I've picked up a casual contract at the hospital," she replied casually.

"I see," Rochelle looked away.

"Just kidding." Chandra thumped Rochelle on the arm. "I wouldn't run off on you to earn a living. I'm going to sit on my butt and spend all your money."

Rochelle pursed her lips. That was not what she wanted either. "Kidding again," Chandra laughed. "I have squillions tucked away. We'll be set for ages provided my cashcard works over here."

"I haven't done too badly myself," she replied, thinking of her vast investment portfolio.

Twenty-Six

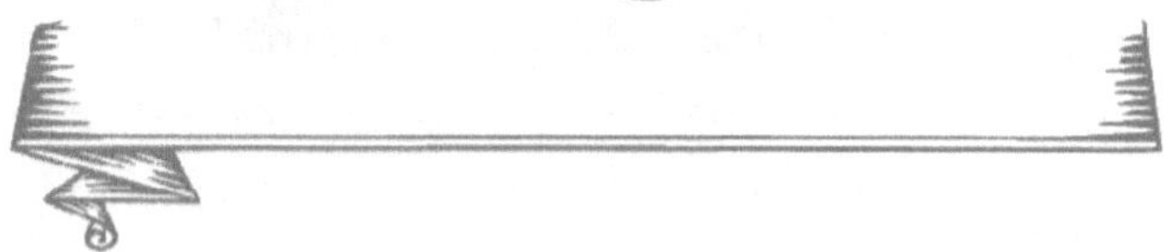

The crystal ball presented the witch with everything she needed to know. Her plan had only rated a ten per cent chance of success. While it would have been great to pull off the coup of the century, the reaping of the boy had not been the point of the exercise. The purpose behind the casting was to give them a chance to study the Gatherers, an annoying group of superhumans that hunted creatures that posed a danger to the humans.

They had not known of the existence of the fairies that worked alongside the Gatherers. That was a piece of information highly valuable to their kind. The magical properties of the fairies would add so much more to their spells and potions than they could gain from the animals in their current arsenal. Their main aim, however, was to be able to harvest human organs for the more complicated curses in their grimoire. To have a clear run at enslaving humans for their magical requirements, the removal of the Gatherers was of the highest priority.

The witch picked up her phone and pushed a button. Numerous texts containing the same message were delivered to witches across the state. She stepped outside the house and scurried to a shed which was situated in the back corner of her property. It was bigger than her home, constructed of corrugated iron and air-conditioned for the comfort of those imprisoned inside.

Four gilded cages stood against the northern wall, each nearing six metres on the diagonal. Another four were situated along the southern wall, the sides rising two and a half metres above floor level and constructed from the same floor plan as their counterparts. Inside each was a child between the ages of five and eight.

The witch walked over to a small cream box situated at face level near the entrance. "Children, your food will be delivered shortly. You will have fifteen minutes to consume your meal and take care of your toileting needs before being released for your daily exercise."

She moved to a fridge and took out the containers her brother had prepared earlier. She growled in anger at the care and expense he had gone to when fixing their meals. He was a waste of space as far as she was concerned. There was no need for them to eat restaurant-quality food for what she had in mind for them. Most of the time they wasted their energy by begging to be reunited with their parents. Ungrateful little sods. They had a comfortable bed to sleep on, their own bathroom – which they wouldn't have if she had not taken them from their parents, and three more-than-adequate meals a day. What more could a child want from a carer?

She carried the containers to a compartment in the wall, opened the door, and dumped one of the containers. Once the door was closed, she pressed a button that allowed the chamber to be accessed from the other side. She repeated this process until all eight children had access to their food. Once the children had collected their meal, she pushed another set of buttons and walked to the opposite corner of the structure. She opened the door of a tall, thin cupboard and pulled out a state-of-the-art hazmat suit. After putting the protective clothing on over the top of her current outfit, she sat on a chair and waited for what was to come.

The scraping of cutlery against the plastic and the flushing of toilets grated on her nerves. She was impatient to get the next portion of their plan underway. The hissing of gas nozzles spitting to life brought a smile to her craggy old face. She cackled with laughter as the sounds of their screams reached her ears. The witch was unconcerned by their reactions. She had honed the process to perfection. The remnants of her failed subjects provided food for the herbs and vegetables grown in the garden outside.

She knew the process was finished when the alarm she had set earlier blared inside the restricted space. The witch walked to the viewing pane of the closest child's cage and felt happy with the result. She hurried through her appraisal of the other children and sent another text to the group. The button was pressed on the intercom, and she addressed her new army of soldiers.

"Children, you have arrived at a new stage in your development. Please make your way to the mirror to see what you have become."

The clang of broken glass echoed throughout the building. The witch took out a notebook from a drawer along the wall and began to take notes.

- All children have successfully transformed.
- Anger levels are at a maximum.
- Creatures have a gruesome appearance.

She addressed them again, "I am going to open your doors. You will stand outside your room and await further instructions. Failure to do so will be punished severely."

The doors slid open, and the newly-transformed creatures stepped outside. Their angry faces glared at the witch, though they pressed their backs against the walls of their prison. "What have you done to us?" the eldest one asked.

"Made you stronger," the witch answered, making another note in her book.

• Follows instructions

"What are we?" asked another.

"My soldiers," the witch answered.

"What are we?" the creature asked again, the pitch of its voice rising higher.

The witch looked up distractedly. "Trolls," she answered, realising what the creature meant. "You have been subjected to several compounds to enable your transformation, one of which is the DNA extracted from a troll. I love it when science and magic come together." She rubbed her hands together with boundless enthusiasm.

"Why would you do this to us?" the eldest asked, taking a step forward.

"Back to your post," the witch warned. "I've already told you – to make you stronger."

"For what purpose?" another whined. "Why can't we go home?"

"You can go home when you get rid of the Gatherers."

"What is a Gatherer?" the youngest creature asked.

"I will show you pictures and tell you where you can find them. If you kill them, I will turn you back into children and send you home to your parents."

"Really?" the eldest asked sceptically.

"Promise," the witch said, unsure of their ability to get the job done.

"When do we get started?"

"Now," the witch confirmed.

The witch retrieved the photos she had received from some of her coven members. She had printed them out and placed them in a binder. She showed them to the trolls with an explanation of how to find them. "They have begun congregating together. It is an unusual practice for the Gatherers, who usually work on their own. There has never been a better time for you to take them out."

"How are we supposed to do that?"

The witch looked at their oversized teeth and their wickedly extended claws. "I have given you all the tools you will need. Let instinct be your guide when you spot your prey. Do this well, children, and you will be home in your own beds in no time."

"I can't kill a person," the youngest troll whined.

"You can if you want to see your parents again," the eldest troll answered.

The witch sat down with them and went over her plan, then opened the door to the outside. The sun felt a lot cooler than usual when it hit their new roughened skin. The light hurt their eyes, and they squinted against its brightness. The witch had wanted them to split into two groups; one going after Force and April, the other hunting down Rochelle and Chandra.

The eldest listened to his gut which told him they would have more success if they stayed together. After listening to the witch, he knew Rochelle and Chandra were on the lookout for something out of the ordinary. He decided they would have more luck by starting their attack with April and Force who were unaware of the witches and would be unprepared for the arrival of the witch's army.

His grin was terrifying. "We are coming for you, Gatherers," he shouted to the delight of the others, who fed off his menace, empowering themselves. They would not be in this predicament if it weren't for the Gatherers. The trolls channelled their fury into action as they located the position of the sun to ascertain their bearings, then sprinted in the direction of Force's new accommodation.

Titles by Marnie Atwell

Starlight Investigations

Jealousy Monsters

Vampire

Phantasm

Halloween Madness

The Pumpkin Patch

The House of Horrors

The Spirited Scarecrow

About the Author

Marnie is an Australian author who lives in South-East Queensland with her husband and two children. When she is not dreaming up new adventures for her characters, Marnie enjoys creating pictures with Daz 3D; reading paranormal romance novels; playing the piano; and spending quality time with family and friends. Not necessarily in that order.

Visit her website at: www.marnieatwell.com for more books, contact details, and free downloads.

The next book in the Starlight Investigation series is:
Trolls